After the Blackout

a Novel

by Paul Anthony

Published by:

Voltaire Publishing Company
www.voltairepress.com

Requests to the publisher for permission should be addressed to: permissions@voltairepress.com

ISBN: 978-0-9773092-2-1 (E-book)

ISBN: 978-0-9773092-3-8 (paperback)

Table of contents:

Preface

To most people, it came as a surprise.

It shouldn't have. All the indications were there. Everything we depended on in our lives relied on electricity, and the grids were old, overloaded and vulnerable.

Oh, sure, politicians talked about "investing" in infrastructure, and "investing " in renewable energy sources, and becoming "energy self-sufficient ". But that was just political rhetoric. Everyone that knew anything, knew that we wouldn't be able to provide enough energy for the ever- increasing demand. And those who REALLY knew also knew any power grid, whether it was fed by coal or oil or nuclear or even solar or wind, would be vulnerable to an EMP blast. And that could come from a nuclear explosion or massive solar flares. Either way, it was going to happen eventually. It was just a matter of time.

And yet, when the time came, most everyone was surprised.

I blame Hollywood for that. There had been more than a few apocalyptic movies and TV shows that had conditioned us to think we knew what it would be like. They were wrong. Of course, Hollywood's role is to entertain us, not to prepare us for reality. We went to the movies to *escape* reality. Even "reality" shows weren't real.

But we sat in the theaters and watched as the actors pretended to react to what the writers thought we wanted to believe. The way most of the stories went, everything would be normal and then the lights would flicker and fade. We would watch as all the lights in the city went out one by one, cascading across the horizon. All the movies showed it happening the same way, so I suppose we thought we knew how it would be.

Well, that's not what happened. Nobody got to watch the city go dark, because it happened at 7:35 AM. I suppose people in stores or in office buildings might have seen the lights go out, but we were used to temporary power outages by then, so they didn't realize what had *really* happened.

For most people, the first indication was when their smart phones went stupid.

And, for many people, the biggest inconvenience was that they knew *something* was happening but they couldn't 'tweet' about it. It took a few days for the realization to sink in. The lights weren't coming back on!

By then, everything had changed. Most people never learned why it happened, because most people didn't live long enough to find out. Those that survived stopped asking why. They were too busy surviving.

Chapter 1 – Lone Survivor - Day One

It was 8:35 AM when Mike stepped out of the shower. Sleeping in on Sundays was a luxury he enjoyed for many years, and this was just another Sunday.

Some people might think he lived a dull life, but at the ripe old age of fifty-nine, dull suited him. He still went to work Monday through Friday. Saturdays were consumed by necessary chores like cleaning and laundry after his ritualistic meeting with a few friends at the local coffee shop. But Sunday was his day of rest, with nothing scheduled and no one to meet with or deal with. He had earned this "dull" routine, and he savored it.

It hadn't always been this way. When he was younger, Sunday mornings were all about family. His wife saw to that. But Maria passed away three years ago, shortly after the kids had moved out to raise their own families. Now it was just Mike and his dog Plato enjoying the solitude – at least on Sundays. No meetings, no TV, no internet and the phone turned off. Peace at last.

So, at 8:42, after slipping into comfortable clothes that were nothing like the sort he wore during the week, he went downstairs and poured a cup of coffee. It looked like a nice December day – sunny, with the high temperature predicted to be in the sixties – so he stepped out onto the patio to enjoy a cigarette. His dog followed him out, but with something else on his mind.

Normally, it would be very quiet. Most of his neighbors were church-goers, so there should have been no one around, but he could hear a lot of anxious chatter from all directions. Something was wrong. Plato sensed it, too.

A quick look around didn't tell him anything. Of course, with six-foot block fences surrounding every yard in this suburban Arizona neighborhood, looking around didn't do much good. But the sky was clear in all directions, so there couldn't be a fire. Besides, Plato would have detected a fire faster than Mike. Plato was still sniffing the air.

"What do you think it is, Plato?"

Apparently, Plato hadn't come to any conclusions yet. You can't rush an expert.

Mike could venture out and ask someone, but this was Sunday and what good is a Sunday if you have to talk to people? If Maria were still alive, she would have been out there with them – or invited them in for coffee. They had made a good team. Maria was definitely an extrovert and Mike was the opposite. When the kids came home for the funeral, Mike Junior insisted his Dad get a dog for companionship because he was concerned that Mike would become even more withdrawn. He was probably right.

So, although Mike wanted to know what had his neighbors upset, it just wasn't in his nature to socialize. No, it would be easier to turn on the TV and catch the news that's aired twenty-four hours a day. So, Mike left Plato to continue his investigation and went inside.

The TV produced nothing. One-hundred and eighty-something channels, and nothing on any of them. The cable must be out. That happens sometimes, but that can't be what has everyone upset. OK, time to boot up the computer and check for news on-line.

Most people accessed the net via their smart phones or tablets, but Mike wasn't interested in being connected 24-7. He still had a desktop PC and an old cell phone that only made phone calls (it also had a camera, but he wasn't interested in taking pictures, either). On Sundays, neither the PC nor the phone was turned on, so he had to wait for the computer to boot before he could launch a browser. "Site not found". Hmm... Then he noticed there were none of the usual annoying flashing lights on the modem.

Reluctantly, he picked up his land-line phone to call a friend. The phone was dead, too. Well, sure, the phone, internet and TV were all fed by the same cable company. They must be having a local outage. "Where is that infernal cell phone", he muttered. After turning it on and waiting a minute, it displayed "no signal".

"Ok Mike, think...what could interfere with both cable and cell reception" he said, as if asking aloud would get a faster answer. Well, sometimes it worked. The answer came to him and he blurted it out. "A power outage - one big enough to affect the Cable Company and local cell towers". He had installed solar panels a few years back, so he still had electricity, but his neighbors wouldn't. That would explain all that anxious chatter he'd heard. Well, he had prepared for this and he knew there were steps he needed to take to conserve energy.

Charging up his twelve batteries during the day usually got him through the night at this time of year, but he'd kept a connection to the grid in case the batteries got low. Mostly, he relied on the grid in the summer months for the AC. It wasn't an 'off-the-grid' system, but it also wasn't what the power company tried to sell him. They wanted him to sell his excess power to them during the day and then buy it back at night. If he had let them talk him into that, his solar system would have automatically turned off when they had an outage. What sense would that make?

It was a sunny day, so the batteries would charge just fine, but he figured he ought to turn off any unnecessary stuff. Since he'd already showered, he didn't need to keep the water heater on.

Plato had given up his investigation outside, preferring to see what Mike was up to. When Mike shut off the thermostat, he explained his actions to his dog. "No point in risking the central heat coming on when it's such a beautiful day, Plato. You probably prefer fresh air anyway". He opened as many windows as could be opened. Many of them were not built to open. These new 'energy efficient' homes were designed with central air in mind. The architects and engineers thought it more efficient to let the heat pump maintain the temperature, and they didn't want people choosing to let in outside air at the wrong times.

Over the years, government and special interest lobbyists like environmentalists had slowly but incrementally reduced the choices people could make for themselves. The "nanny state" thought it knew best, but here was an example of how those seemingly great ideas proved to be wrong. Thinking about it just irritated him, as usual, so he put the thoughts out of his mind and tried to focus on the next appropriate course of action. He needed to know more about what happened and how long it might last. That's why he had a battery-powered short-wave radio.

"This isn't good" he mumbled, as he slowly turned the dial, finding...*nothing!*

Although he had prepared for something like this, he didn't welcome it. If this was as wide-spread as it seemed, some very nasty things were going to happen over the next few days and if they were going to survive, they would need to keep a low profile. He had read a lot about "preppers" and all the steps they took to prepare for any kind of emergency. Some of them sounded paranoid, but Mike had installed solar panels and stocked up on canned goods that had a long shelf-life, just in case.

Some of his neighbors knew he had installed a solar array. He had been careful to make it inconspicuous and was, for once, grateful for the Homeowners Association's rules that practically demanded it, but he couldn't keep the construction a secret. They knew. If the power didn't come back on soon, someone was going to get envious. With a little luck, they had forgotten. "Life is full of irony, Plato. We have electricity, but I don't dare turn on the lights tonight". Plato nodded in agreement.

It wasn't just the electricity that might tempt his neighbors. When people get hungry, they get dangerous. For too many people, dinner is something you pick up at the drive-thru window. Those will be shut soon. Stores will be looted. When all the food is gone off the shelves, people might turn on their neighbors. He had stockpiled quite a bit of food and water, but not enough to feed the whole neighborhood. He owned a gun, but didn't relish having to use it.

He could think of nothing else to do but wait. Maybe the power will come back on, and everything will go back to normal. Mike pulled a book from the shelf and settled down to enjoy his favorite pastime. Plato relaxed a little, too, but remained ever watchful.

The day passed as most Sundays did. Mike checked the short wave radio occasionally. The power was still out everywhere, but it hadn't prevented him from enjoying his day off. As the sun began to set, Mike closed the few windows he had opened and checked the bank of batteries in the garage to be sure his conservation efforts had worked. He had plenty of power to keep the refrigerator running through the night and to run a space heater to fend off the cold. None of his neighbor's Christmas lights were coming on as they usually did and there were no street lights. If he turned on any of his lights, his house would stand out like a Christmas tree, so he went to bed when it got too dark to read.

Chapter 2 – Day two

As soon as the sun rose, Mike was awake. The first hint of dawn was a stark contrast to the complete darkness of the night before. Normally, even with the blinds closed and the drapes drawn tight there was some light in the bedroom. Not last night! Mike wondered if that was why he had slept so soundly. Or, maybe it was because he had gone to bed so damn early! This was how people used to live before electric lights were invented. "Early to bed, early to rise, makes a man...*grumpy!*" he said to Plato, who was always ready for another day no matter what time it started.

Since he had power, he couldn't know if the blackout was over so he tried the short-wave again. *Nothing.* Well, there was no point in going to the office. He stepped into the shower and regretted turning off the water heater. The water was very *c-o-l-d!* It had seemed like a good idea yesterday, but maybe he'd conserved too much. He dressed quickly. It was Monday, but since he wasn't going anywhere he didn't bother to shave. Shaving with cold water might be hazardous to his health. Well, he'd enjoy an extended weekend.

He hadn't turned off the automatic timer on the coffee maker, but it was set for a more reasonable hour so he had to start it manually and wait for his morning brew. Plato didn't want to wait, so Mike let him out and stepped outside with him. His neighbors were up, too, and they were chattering much like they were yesterday.

Mike didn't know any of them well. If Maria were still alive, she would have invited everyone over within the first few weeks after they moved in, but Mike bought this house after she passed away and he didn't feel very sociable at the time. In fact he only knew a few of his neighbors by name, so it wasn't surprising that no one had come over. That was fine, because he didn't want to remind anyone that he was better prepared than they were. He was going to keep quiet about it as long as possible.

And then the doorbell rang.

"Shit. Doorbells aren't supposed to work in a power outage" he thought as he peeked through the peephole. It was Kayla, one of the few neighbors he actually knew by name. *"Well, no sense pretending I'm not here because she probably saw me opening the windows yesterday"*. So he opened the door and was greeted by his neighbor.

"Hi, Mike. Bill and I were just wondering if you were okay." she said in her usual cheerful manner.

"Well, yeah, I'm fine considering...What happened?"

"Nobody seems to know" she said, still smiling. Mike wondered if there was anything that could ever be bad enough to make her stop smiling. She continued, "Everybody's packing up, getting ready to head up north. If you're ready, you could join our little caravan. You are going, aren't you?" she asked.

"No, I'm not leaving yet. Thanks for asking. Thank Bill for me."

And then she was gone, apparently oblivious to the mystery of why the doorbell worked. "Good thing Bill didn't come himself. He would have asked. And I thought I was prepared. What else did I neglect to think about?" Mike asked Plato, as he got the step ladder and proceeded to pull the wires off the wall-mounted ringer.

Although the doorbell had freaked him out, Mike was relieved by the news that people were leaving town. Keeping a low profile would be a lot easier with no one around. Most of his neighbors had second homes in the mountains. Mike just had this house, and he planned on staying put. There was nothing left to do but wait out the outage – if it was temporary. He had his doubts about that. What could have caused it?

He thought it might have been an EMP. He'd read about electro-magnetic pulses, which could be caused by an atomic blast or by solar flares, but everything he'd read seemed to imply that everything electrical would be fried. But his neighbors' cars weren't affected. Maybe what he'd heard had been exaggerated. People who talked about such things usually made it sound worse than it would be because they were usually trying to panic people into buying something.

From what Mike knew about electricity, it is possible that an EMP would blow out all the transformers and maybe burn anything that had current running through it, but any device that wasn't connected might be spared. Everything in his house was working. His solar array wasn't damaged. If it hit just before sunrise, there would have been no electricity running through the system. That might explain that.

Everyone kept their cars in their garages, and most people weren't driving early on a Sunday morning. Anyone who was on the road wouldn't be so lucky. What if another flare occurs while they're on the road? People just don't think. Mike was even more certain the best plan was to stay put.

Well, there wasn't much else he could do now but wait. His

mind wandered to thoughts of his children and grand children. He had been encouraging them to prepare for an emergency like this, but they – like most people these days – thought his talk of a total collapse of civilization was just the ramblings of an old man approaching senility. How would they survive this? Would they try to come home? They lived two-thousand miles away. Was travelling that far even possible?

For the first time, Mike, who relished his solitude, was lonely.

Chapter 3 – Week Five

"Well, we got through four whole weeks and the sun is shining. So far, so good" Mike said to Plato, as he marked another day off the calendar. But it hadn't been all that good. Christmas had been tough. Holidays without family around just aren't holidays! They were supposed to be together at Mike's house this Christmas. Even though it seemed obvious no one was coming, he had kept the tree up and the gifts under it until the first of January. Putting it all away was difficult, but looking at it all every day had started to feel like a memorial service. They might still be alive, but...

The worst part was that he had so much time to think! Although Mike had always been an avid reader, he had quite a few books that there had never been enough time to read. Getting caught up on his passion for books passed a lot of time, but it was still hard not to think.

The last two days provided some relief from that. It had rained for two days, which was good and bad. His food supply was still adequate, but water was scarce and the rains provided a chance to replenish his stock. Collecting run-off, filtering and treating it and filling bottles had kept him very busy. That was good. The bad part was rainy days meant little sunshine, which meant very little solar power. Despite his efforts to conserve, the batteries were almost drained! Today, the sun was shining. That was good.

No one had come to his door since Kayla rang the bell on that first day. He hadn't ventured out beyond his own yard, but there were no sounds of life. This was what would be considered an upper-middle class suburban neighborhood, so it was not surprising that there hadn't been any looters. Like Bill and Kayla, most of the people living around him had probably headed north to escape the blackout. Mike wondered if they had managed to get very far, or if there was anywhere to escape *to*. There was still nothing on the short wave. This had to be very wide-spread!

So, keeping a low profile had been easy. Mike was certain that was the best course of action, but it had been a lonely four weeks. He was getting close to the point where the benefit of finding other survivors might outweigh the risk. Besides, treating all that rain water had consumed most of his chemicals, and he was going to have to find more.

Was there any government effort to provide assistance? After Hurricane Katrina, it had taken a while for rescue operations to reach the devastated area from neighboring states, but what if there was no one in any neighboring states? What if there was no government at all? Mike had never sought government assistance before, so he hadn't planned on relying on the government now.

"We can't stay here forever, and the cavalry is probably not coming to our rescue" Mike said to Plato. He had been talking to his dog – or to himself - a lot lately, not that he wasn't perfectly capable of thinking without speaking, but it had been so quiet! Some people think talking to yourself is a sign of insanity, but the sound of his own voice was the only thing keeping him sane.

He had given a lot of thought to this impending trip. The car's tank was nearly full, and even if the battery was dead it would be easy to jump-start it from the bank of batteries that sat on shelves in the garage right above the hood. The Caddy was 15 years old, but he had kept it in good condition.

And he was pretty sure it would run, despite all the stories about cars being disabled by an EMP blast. His neighbors had all left, so cars were still working. His would be, too, once he recharged the battery. He wasn't worried about the car.

But he was worried about a few other things. What if all the stores had been looted or worse – burned to the ground? What if there were still looters roaming the streets waiting to pounce on anyone who had anything of value? He had sat in his yard every day, listening for any sound that might indicate a threat. Now there was nothing but the sound of birds. They weren't the usual, pleasant sounding birds. These were larger, and menacing. He'd heard dogs howling until about a week ago, which upset Plato more than it upset Mike, but even they were quiet now. *Or dead.*

"I know I can't be the only survivor". Mike mused. *"Plenty of people had the good sense to prepare. I just don't know if any of them live around here"*. Most of those people he had read about on the blogs lived in rural areas, or planned to move to a rural area. They wanted to be able to hunt for food. There wasn't much wild game roaming around in the desert, so preppers were more likely in northern Arizona. It was pretty well understood that survival in or even near a big city would be a pipe dream.

This wasn't a big city, but it was close to one. Until about ten years ago, this was a sleepy little town. But the urban sprawl had reached this far out, and a lot of new homes had been built during the real estate boom on what had been ranches and farms. Mike bought his home right after the boom went bust – when the prices had come back down to earth. Like his neighbors, he was a city boy. But unlike most of them, he wasn't wealthy. He had worked for everything he had, and worked in a lot of different fields. He knew how to do things his neighbors had to hire others to do. He had installed the solar array himself, and knew how to maintain it. He wasn't exactly a prepper, but he would survive. It bothered him that he was acting as paranoid as those people had sounded, but maybe they were right!

But the preppers weren't the only ones prepared. Mormons believed in self-sufficiency and instructed all the members of their church to keep something like six month's worth (or was it a year's worth?) of food in the house. The ranchers and farmers that were here first were mostly Mormons. Mike had talked to a few of them – they referred to themselves as "LDS" – that went door-to-door looking for converts. He loved a good discussion about religion or politics, and had encouraged them to come back again. He knew he wasn't going to change their minds any more than they were going to change his, but he enjoyed the repartee. And although he wouldn't join their church, he respected their life-style. There were a lot of Mormons in this area, although not in his subdivision. They probably survived.

The problem with suburbia was that these subdivisions were full of nothing but houses. He'd have to leave his quiet surroundings and travel a few miles past some *other* subdivisions to reach the stores, mostly all clustered around the freeway on-ramps. And he had no way of knowing what he'd find there until he got there.

Well, he'd find out tomorrow. Today, he'd rest while the batteries recharged.

Chapter 4 – The Journey

The next morning looked promising. The sun was bright, and the sky cloudless. Mike rose at sun-up and showered. The water had stopped flowing...two or three weeks ago? He couldn't remember exactly, but he had to make do. He had filled one of the bathtubs right after the blackout and had rigged up a shower using the recirculating pump from a decorative fountain. Since he hadn't changed the water, it didn't get him any cleaner, but it was still refreshing – although still too cold. Mike had been determined to keep things as "normal" as possible. It would be easy to get lazy and just wallow in self-pity. That would lead to depression and, eventually, to death. Still, he had been lax in some ways. This morning, he shaved, which hadn't seemed worth the effort lately. But today was different. He might meet someone, and he didn't want to scare them off. He dressed the way he used to when he worked, and went downstairs.

Mike continued his morning ritual. "Breakfast" was a scoop of some energy powder he had bought a few cases of, mixed in a tall glass of cold coffee. Not bad, but it used to taste better with milk. Then he poured a scoop of kibble in the bowl for Plato, who always waited patiently for Mike to drink his breakfast first. Next, his morning bowel movement meant going out in the yard, opening the five-gallon bucket and placing the toilet seat on it. This would never seem 'normal', but the toilets didn't flush and it wouldn't be sanitary to leave human waste in the house. His parent's generation grew up using outhouses, and they survived.

He would survive, too, but he didn't have to like it!

Most people used to think the loss of electricity would be the biggest challenge, but it turned out that the lack of running water and flush toilets was what presented the greatest inconvenience. But for Plato, life *was* normal. While Mike squatted in one corner of the yard, Plato did the same in the opposite corner, as he always had. You can't miss what you never had.

Mike stepped into the garage and checked the batteries. They were nearly charged to capacity, and they would reach the max soon enough. Then he went to the kitchen and filled some water bottles, checked that the Glock was loaded and grabbed a flash light and a battery powered lantern. He was as ready and as presentable as he could be. It was time to explore the world, or at least that small portion of the world that could be reached with one tank-full of gas.

"Come on, Plato, we're going for a ride!" Plato hadn't heard that phrase in a very long time, but he hadn't forgotten its meaning. He was standing at the door to the garage before Mike got there.

Mike backed the car out of the garage and waited. No one approached him. After closing the garage door, he drove slowly around the block. It had always been a quiet neighborhood, but this was eerily quiet. Then, he drove out to the main road, stopping at the stop sign and then chuckling at himself. There was no traffic, but old habits die hard.

He headed north, toward the freeway. There was a major grocery store about a mile south of the on-ramp, and a big-box home improvement store across the intersection. The mall was further north, but Mike wasn't shopping for clothes. If the market wasn't completely emptied, he might find some chemicals and maybe even some canned goods there. If not, there were some smaller shops surrounding it.

Mike stopped the car and stared in shock. The intersection in front of him was filled with the mangled remains of cars and trucks, most of them burned out hulks. Even worse, there were the charred remains of...*people!*

He could see that the stores around the intersection were not just empty. They had been gutted by fire. Although it was a senseless thing to do, he let Plato out of the car and they walked through the carnage, unable to accept the total devastation his eyes confirmed.

Wandering aimlessly now, they reached the overpass and looked down on the freeway. All of the lanes were full of bumper-to-bumper traffic, except the traffic wasn't moving. People had tried to leave Phoenix, and had gotten nowhere. There were vehicles as far as he could see, all stopped. A lot of car doors were open, indicating that people had given up waiting and had decided to walk out, but how far could they have gotten? Looking down from his high perch, he could see bodies between the cars. There were probably more inside the cars. One thing was for sure. Nothing and no one was moving.

How could this happen? As soon as that question popped into his head, the answer was obvious. In their panic to get away, there would be accidents. Traffic would back up. Cell phones didn't work so no one could call for a tow-truck, not that any tow-trucks drivers would be waiting for a call. Everyone was desperately trying to leave. So, traffic would slow down, and someone would run out of gas. That would clog the road even more. There were just too many people. Or at least there used to be too many people.

He stood there for a long time, not sure what to do next. Every option he could think of seemed futile. Could he be the only survivor? That was just inconceivable... How long could he continue to survive? *And how much longer would he want to?*

"Okay, enough of this! You were smarter than they were, which is why you're still alive and they're not, so are you gonna just give up now?" There's nothing like a good pep talk, even if you have to give it to yourself. "Think, damn it! These stores are right near the freeway, so you should have known they would be looted. We need to go to the smaller markets, ones in residential neighborhoods, away from the main roads". He had shopped at a local store occasionally, but had preferred the major chain stores because they were cheaper. But money was no object now.

Mike and Plato walked back to the car quickly. Although Mike was never a fan of horror movies, there was something foreboding about this scene. If he let his imagination loose, he could almost see ghosts and zombies emerging from the wreckage. That was nonsense, but there was no harm in walking just a little faster, or maybe jogging. Hey, Plato needed the exercise, right?

Once they were back in the car, he realized how ridiculous that had been. He hadn't exerted himself that much in at least a month and he was winded. Plato was panting, too. So they shared some water and rested for a few minutes before starting the car.

It was about four miles to the small market, and there were no burned-out cars to avoid along the way. The carnage hadn't reached this part of town, but that didn't mean things were normal. There was no traffic and no cars in the parking lot of the strip mall. The doors to the market were unlocked, but of course the lights were off.

When he opened the door, the smell nearly took his breath away. A lot of frozen foods and fresh produce had spoiled. Plato refused to go any further, and Mike couldn't blame him. Mike put Plato back in the car, took a deep breath and went inside the store. Flashing the light around, he saw something he should have expected, but hadn't. *Rats!* Well, of course! They were nature's garbage collectors, and they had a lot of work to do in here.

"I never really enjoyed shopping, but this is ridiculous!" He debated with himself. "I really need some chemicals, and canned goods don't spoil. I really should go back in there and get some food". Still, it had been irrational to imagine zombies, but these rats were real. If he was bitten, how would he treat his wounds? What if they were rabid? Nope, going back in would be too risky.

While he thought about what he would do if he was injured, he glanced around and noticed a drug store a few doors down. "They probably sell everything I'm looking for, but they don't sell produce, so there shouldn't be much in there that could spoil. It would be a good idea to get some kind of antiseptic, in case I ever do need it". The drug store was a much better choice. Again the door was unlocked. People had just walked away everywhere! Or, more likely, security was electronic. We had come to rely on computers to handle so many things we used to do manually. They probably couldn't lock the doors when the power went out.

Mike opened the door cautiously. There was no obnoxious odor, so he went in and did his shopping. It had always been his habit to mentally tally up the prices of everything he put in his cart, so when he was finished he knew about what the tab should be. Of course there was no one manning the checkout counter, but Mike placed some cash next to the register. "I'm no looter" he announced, to no one in particular.

Plato was happy to see him when he reached the car, and Mike was happy their journey was almost over. Staying home would seem less tedious after today's experience. Before Mike could close the car door, Plato growled, then barked and leapt out of the car, running. "Hey! What the heck has gotten into you? Get back here! *Plato!*"

Chapter 5 – Alone no more

Plato kept running. Mike pulled the Glock from its holster and followed him, walking, not running this time. He remembered what running felt like from before. Fortunately, he didn't have far to go. Plato had stopped and was barking. As Mike approached, he could see a body on the ground next to Plato.

The body wasn't moving, but Mike approached cautiously, looking around for any accomplices. This could be a trap. The body might have been placed here to lure him, and while his guard was down someone would jump him. He hadn't always been this cynical, but times had changed. "Plato, I think I'm becoming paranoid. There's no one in sight and no place nearby where anyone could be hiding. If this is a trap, it isn't a very good one."

Then the body groaned.

It was a woman, maybe in her forty's, dirty but alive and alone. How did she get here? Still wary, Mike knelt down and offered her some water. She drank a little, but choked on it. After coughing so hard that her whole body convulsed, she composed herself and reached for the bottle while whispering what sounded like "Thank you".

Less suspicious now, Mike helped her sit up and allowed her to sip some more water. Her clothes were not inexpensive - what might be called business casual. Her face bore the remnants of makeup and her hair, although dirty, appeared to have been professionally cut and had been previously dyed. She had wanted to be an ash blonde, but her roots disclosed a natural tendency toward dark brown with a touch of gray. All that, combined with the size of the wedding ring on her delicate hand implied that she and her husband belonged in this neighborhood.

So, where was her husband? Mike looked around again, distrust outweighing his compassion. No, she was definitely alone and not in very good shape, from the looks of it. Mike was no doctor, but he suspected she hadn't had much food or water for awhile. "Well, you're alive. I can't just leave you here, but what am I going to do with you?"

He didn't like being out in the open like this, exposed to...*what? Who knows!* "Stay here while I get the car", he said, as if she was going to get up and go anywhere. Plato stayed by her side while Mike walked back to the car. *"What a fool I've been"* he thought. *"While I was tending to her, someone could have made off with the Caddy".* It was a good thing it wasn't a trap, because Mike was just not cut out for that sort of intrigue. *"The car's still here, so stop imagining the worst. The poor woman needs help, and there's no one else here to help her, so I guess I'd better come up with a plan".*

When he drove up next to Plato and the woman, she seemed to be feeling better. The water had definitely helped, but she probably needed to eat something. The canned goods he had "purchased" didn't have pop-tops, and he didn't have a can opener with him, so they would have to go back to the house. Still, Mike wasn't sure he wanted to show anyone where he lived or what he had there.

"Listen, I have a few questions before we go any further", he said as he helped her into the front seat. Plato seemed okay with that, and gladly jumped in the back. "My name is Mike and this is Plato. What's your name?"

"Olivia. My friends call me Liv". Mike's quirky sense of humor kicked in and he couldn't resist saying "Well you <u>did</u> live. It's a good thing your name isn't Diane. Your friends might have called you Di". She laughed. She actually laughed at that corny attempt at humor! Mike thought he could get to like this woman.

"Okay, Liv, tell me how you ended up in an empty parking lot. Where are you from, and where's your husband?"

She started crying. Mike waited. It wasn't that he didn't feel sorry for her, but he needed some answers before he made any kind of commitment, so he waited until her crying subsided. It was clearly painful for her to think about what had happened, and he could see she was trying to brace herself as she started to tell her story.

"We thought we were prepared. We had enough food for a month. Not enough water, though. When it rained, Steve got up on a ladder to try to attach trash bags to the eaves to catch the water. Our house doesn't have...what do you call them? Rain gutters, I think. We didn't have them, so Steve thought he could make something like that out of trash bags. It was raining hard, and the ladder was slippery. He..." She couldn't go on, but it was easy to imagine the next part. He had fallen off the ladder.

Liv caught her breath and continued. "I had been watching from the doorway. He hit the ground so hard! I remember the water in the puddles splashed up. He wasn't moving. I rushed out, but...the puddle was turning red. He wasn't breathing. I went out into the street yelling for help. Then I started walking. There was nothing else I could do..."

Mike put his arms around her and let her cry. There was nothing else *he* could do.

They sat there for awhile, in each other's arms, saying nothing. When Plato whimpered, Mike wasn't sure if it was a sign of sympathy or impatience but it served as a signal that some action was called for. Mike gently disengaged from the embrace and said "We need to find you some help. Are you a member of any church?"

"No, we are...we *were* spiritual, but we didn't attend any church".

"Same here. There are a lot of Mormons in this town, and I think we should see if we can find any of them. They ought to be willing to help you". Although that sounded like a good plan to Mike, he had no idea how he was going to implement it. Knocking on random doors would probably be futile, and a little dangerous. So he drove to the Mormon Church, hoping someone would be there. Finding it wasn't hard. He had driven past it many times. There were no cars in the parking lot, but odds were most people had run out of gas long ago. They'd probably taken to walking. They used to walk door to door all the time anyway.

"Well, will you look at that?" There were two horses tied up next to the church door. Mike got out of the car and knocked on the door. There was no answer. He knocked louder and called out "Hello, anybody in there?" The door opened a little and Mike found himself facing a rifle barrel.

"Whoa, let's not be hasty! I come in peace". As soon as he said it, he realized how dumb it sounded. *"I come in peace"*. What sci-fi movie did that line come from? He tried a different approach. "There's a woman here who needs some help. Can you help us?"

The door opened wider, showing a youngish woman on the other end of the rifle. "Who are you and what do you want?" she said nervously.

"Hi, my name is Mike and the woman in the car is Liv. I found her lying on the ground and gave her some water, but she needs more than that. Can you help?" As Mike was making his plea, a man appeared behind the girl and said "Step aside, sister, I'll deal with this". To Mike, he said "I'm the Bishop of this Ward. Are you or the woman LDS?"

"Is your compassion reserved only for card-carrying members of your church?" Mike had blurted that out with more sarcasm than he had intended. This was not the way to make friends and influence people, and he really needed this man's help. He tried another tack.

"I'm not a Mormon, uh, not LDS, but I've talked with many of your people over the years. I remember two young girls who approached me outside of my home. When I invited them in, they asked if the lady of the house was present. When I told them there was no lady of the house, they declined my invitation. I understood there reticence to enter my home unescorted, so we spoke outside at great length. I don't feel right taking this poor woman into my home, and I thought you'd understand that. I'm sure she would feel more comfortable with other women. That's why I'm here".

That wasn't why he was here, but the part about the two young Mormon girls was true, and he was hoping the half-truth would work. Just then, 'rifle girl' spoke up. "I remember you. I was one of those girls you spoke with that day. He's telling the truth, Bishop. I remember him as a respectful and courteous man".

"You have quite a good memory. That was at least two years ago". Mike thought it was amazing how events that didn't seem important at the time could be so important later. If we realized how our actions and our words influence others, we'd be a whole lot more careful with what we said to strangers.

The girl replied, "We had a memorable conversation that day. You might remember, Bishop, how I had a lot of questions when I came back that day." And Mike thought, *"Yup, I really should be careful what I say to strangers."*

The Bishop said "Oh, yes, I remember! So, you are the man who challenged her to think so profoundly. Someday I'd like to have a serious theological discussion with you, but now is not the time. Bring your friend in. Let us see what we can do for her."

Mike didn't hesitate. With the girl's help, Mike got Liv out of the car and into the church. "Stay in the car, Plato. I'm not sure they're ready to meet you yet."

The girl introduced herself as Sandra, and explained that she had been studying to be a nurse before the blackout. She had come home from college for the holidays and was not able to return, but she knew enough about medicine to give Liv a passable physical examination.

Finally, Sandra turned to Mike and said "She's exhibiting clear signs of dehydration and malnutrition. The dehydration is treatable, but we are all suffering from some degree of malnutrition. We only have the foods we are able to grow, and I'm afraid our diets are not sufficiently varied. She'll need lots of fluids and bed rest - and, of course, as much food as she can keep down. You'll have to take it slowly. Her stomach has shrunk. That's to be expected."

Mike was getting panicky. She was telling him how to take care of her. She *expected* him to take care of her! "Uh, hold on a minute. I explained how I can't take her home with me. Can't she stay with you?"

The Bishop took Mike aside and said "You say you found her".

"Yes. I didn't know her before a few hours ago."

"Yes, I understand, but you found her and you rescued her. Why did you do that?"

"What else could I do? I couldn't just leave her to die! What would *you* have done?"

"The same as you, I should hope. But it was *you* that rescued her. You did it because you are a responsible, caring individual. Now you must continue to be responsible. You must care for her. That should be obvious. Why would you transfer your responsibility to others?"

Mike was stuck and he knew it. The Bishop had presented a logical argument, and Mike had no logical retort. Still, he had to make one more try. "But Bishop, imagine how the woman must feel, being taken to a strange man's home, alone! Wouldn't it be more appropriate if she stayed with another woman?"

The Bishop chuckled. "Mike, this is the 21st century. We are religious, but we are not prudes. It's true that we try to protect our youth when they venture out to the homes of strangers in their missionary work, but this woman is an adult. Unless I have misjudged you, she doesn't need our protection. Take her home with you and help her regain her strength. After that, if she wants to leave, I trust that you will let her".

So that was it. Mike would have a house guest, like it or not. As they were leaving, Sandra said "I remember the street you live on, but not the exact house. Give me your address, and I will check on Liv tomorrow".

"Thanks, I appreciate that. How about right now? Could you come over and help her get settled in? I'd really appreciate that, and I'm sure Liv would, too." Sandra spoke with the Bishop, and apparently he agreed. "Okay, I'll come with you. The Bishop will bring the horses for our return trip".

Liv fell asleep as soon as the car started moving. Sandra seemed willing to talk, and Mike had a lot of questions about his new-found neighbors. She answered his questions with no hesitation.

There had been one-hundred and ten people in their "Ward" which Mike assumed was similar to a parish. Now, there were only eighty-five. It was their custom to keep a supply of food and water. Mike knew that, but he wondered if they had any way to replenish their supplies. Sandra explained that many of the members of the ward had small farms, and some had wells. They also had wind mills, which produced enough power to keep their refrigerators running and to recharge battery-powered lights. Life was hard, but they shared everything they had and no one went hungry.

To Mike, it sounded like a hippie commune, but he kept quiet. He needed her help, and he didn't want to insult her, although she was probably too young to know what a hippie commune was. Besides, their socialist society had kept them alive, so who was he to object? It was fine for them, but he wasn't going to be a part of it. The important thing was, he knew more about them than they knew about him. Or so he thought.

That changed as soon as Mike pressed the button on the

automatic garage door opener. Sandra let out an audible gasp, as if she had just witnessed a miracle. "You have electricity!" she exclaimed as the overhead light came on, lighting their path into the garage.

"Yeah, I installed solar panels a few years ago. It's enough power for lights and of course, for the refrigerator. On cold nights, I can take the chill out with a space heater. It's not enough to run the central air, though" Mike admitted. Well, what could he do? He had invited her into his home, so he couldn't keep it all a secret.

They got out of the car, but Mike said "Wait here a minute. Plato, let's check the house". Mike had been nervous about leaving the house unprotected and now he let Plato search the house to make sure no one had broken in, while Mike grabbed a large trash bag and a robe. Satisfied that everything was as they had left it, Mike returned to the garage.

"Okay, come on in". He led them into the bathroom that was right next to the back door. "Sandra, please get Liv out of those filthy clothes and put them in this bag. Here's a robe for now. I'll get some clean clothes for her to wear after you get her cleaned up a bit".

"How am I supposed to get her cleaned up? Don't tell me you have running water!"

"No, but I have a kind of a shower upstairs. Get her into this robe, and I'll show you what I mean".

After they came out of the bathroom, Mike led the women upstairs, grabbing some towels from the linen closet and a pair of jeans and a dress shirt from the walk-in on the way to the master bath. He showed them how the recirculating shower worked. "The water isn't very clean, but there's soap, shampoo and conditioner here. I'm sure you'll be cleaner than you are now, Liv. Plato and I will go downstairs and wait for the Bishop".

Before going downstairs, Mike took some clean sheets from the linen closet and laid them on the bed in the guest room. That simple act brought back memories of past visits with his grandkids. Would he ever see them again? He had to stop wondering. With luck, they survived but traveling thousands of miles was simply not possible. With a full tank of gas and ideal driving conditions he could go maybe 400 miles. Then what? There aren't any gas stations operating here, so why should he think there would be any along the way? Besides, he couldn't carry enough food and water for an extended journey of two-thousand miles. No, he couldn't get to them and they couldn't get to him. He could only hope that they were safe.

Mike walked out to the driveway just as the Bishop was untying some sort of bundle from the saddle of the spare horse. "I want you to know, we care for all people, not only for members of our Church. I have brought some fresh produce for you and your guest".

Not to be out done, Mike said "Thanks, it's been a long time since I've had anything fresh. This looks like it would make a good salad. Come on in. I'll cook some pasta and some marinara sauce. We can all enjoy a meal together".

The Bishop looked surprised, but regained his composure and replied "I haven't had pasta in a long time. This will be a treat for both of us!"

So far, so good. If they could cooperate, maybe everyone might benefit - as long as they approached this as equals. Mike was determined to keep the Bishop from getting the upper hand again.

The pot had come to a boil when Sandra and Liv came downstairs, and Sandra couldn't wait to tell the Bishop about the shower. "We must ask him to help us build showers, too. It looked so inviting I almost wanted to get in with Liv". Realizing how that sounded, Sandra blushed. But to Mike, the important thing was that he had scored some points. Let the Bishop top that!

Sandra prepared the salad as Mike cooked the main course, and the four of them sat down for a meal together. Liv wasn't able to eat much, but she seemed to appreciate it. During dinner, the conversation was as polite and congenial as it was inane and empty. No one made any more comments about who had what or who was better off. It was reminiscent of many dinner parties Mike had reluctantly attended when his wife was still alive.

After the meal was consumed and the table cleared, Mike said "Liv, you look tired. Would you like to lie down?"

"Yes, I am tired. I'm afraid I haven't been a very good dinner guest. Thank you for all you've done for me – all of you! If you won't consider it rude, I really would like to rest".

"Of course. Sandra, if I might ask one more thing...I put clean sheets in the guest room but I didn't have time to make the bed. It's the first room on the right at the top of the stairs".

"No problem. Come on, Liv. Let's get you settled in".

Once the women had left the room, there was an awkward silence. Finally, the Bishop turned to Mike and said "You seem to be mechanically inclined. There may be something you could help us with. A few of our brothers have been trying to get the water treatment plant operating. Would you be willing to consult with them?"

"You may be overestimating my skills, but I'd be happy to help in any way I can. Honestly, the thing I miss most is a flush toilet! Are they going to pump the water through the entire town, or just for a few houses?"

"I don't know the details. If you're willing, you could talk to them yourself. They're at the plant soon after sunup every day. The man in charge is called Jonathon. Can I tell him to expect you tomorrow?"

"I'll be there."

Sandra was back. The Bishop said "Good. Well, thanks for dinner. We should be going. We try not to be outside after dark".

Mike walked them out to their horses and they said their final good-byes. He had wanted to ask the Bishop more questions, but thought it best to take this slowly. He'd see what he could learn from Jonathon tomorrow.

After locking up and turning off the lights, Mike went upstairs to check on Liv. Her door was locked. That was just as well. Mike thought he'd lock his own bedroom door tonight, too. She didn't really seem like a threat, but he didn't know much about her.

Then again, what did he know about the Bishop or Sandra? Mike didn't sleep very well that night.

32

Chapter 6 – The Bishop

Joshua had been a bright student, although a little wild. He applied the same energy to his extra-curricular activities as he did to his studies. Not that he ever did anything wrong. He just lived life to its fullest, within the limitations imposed by his religion. He didn't drink or smoke, but there weren't many restrictions on having sex.

The elders had some concerns, but he was smart and they never had reason to question his devotion to faith. And so, after Joshua completed his mission and graduated from Brigham Young University they named him Bishop of his local Ward. He was the youngest to have received the honor.

Everything seemed to come easy for "Josh", as he preferred to be called when he was younger. But that was a façade he had carefully constructed. Underneath, he was a perfectionist who was never quite satisfied with himself. He did well in school because he wouldn't settle for anything less. When it was time to perform his mission, he did more than was expected of him by others – but everything that he expected from himself.

When he was named Bishop, he accepted the honor with humility, but never doubted that he deserved it. The position was for two years. Josh was anxious to get started, but equally anxious for it to be over. This would just be another phase in his life that had to be dutifully performed before he could move on to the next phase. As with every other endeavor, Josh knew he would perform his new duties admirably.

It would not be a difficult job. He would have some oversight regarding the budget, but there were others who did most of that work. His primary responsibility would be to provide spiritual guidance to the members of his Ward, and Josh knew he was well qualified. Despite all his other interests, he had a thorough understanding of the Holy Texts.

Two weeks after he assumed his new duties, the power went out. And the world changed.

Josh had not really noticed the diversity within the Ward. There were the old families that had founded the town and there were the new-comers who shared the same faith but lived...*differently*. These differences had irritated the elders, but Josh had been oblivious to the friction. Sure, he knew the old families were predominantly ranchers while the new arrivals lived in modern suburban homes with minimal yard space. And maybe he was aware of subtle aversions cast by each toward the others, but that was a problem for the older generation. He and his classmates in High School had gotten along fine. But now, those differences were becoming more apparent.

No longer satisfied with spiritual guidance, the Church members looked to Josh for leadership in every aspect of their lives. The greatest conflict arose over the allocation of resources. The LDS Church instructed its followers to store ample food and water in case of emergency, but Josh was surprised to find how many had not done so. Those that hadn't complied with the edict had turned to the Church, expecting to be fed. The ranchers had land and the knowledge needed to raise crops. Others had neither the land nor the expertise.

It had become Josh's responsibility to settle the dispute that was threatening to divide his Church! As was his custom, he prayed for guidance, but it was almost as if God's light had gone out when Man's lights failed. His faith was not shaken, really, but he was not getting answers. Perhaps God was testing him. No, not testing. More like challenging him to use his own initiative. Left to his own resources, Josh was grateful for the education he had received. He had majored in Political Science. He knew something about governmental theory, and he would apply that knowledge here.

The problem, as he saw it, was an ideological clash between the conservative nature of the Church as interpreted by the old families and the more liberal view shared by the newer families. He tended to side with the liberals, as his University studies had always conflicted with his family's politics.

But Josh was determined to resolve this in a way that would best represent his theological beliefs. *"Am I not my brother's keeper?"* he asked himself. *"How can I deny any of the brethren in their time of need?"* The proper direction was clear. He remembered this famous quote: "From each according to his ability, to each, according to his need". But convincing the farmers to share their crops with others had proved to be difficult.

Getting the water flowing again was going to help ease some of that tension. The farmers would be more willing to provide food for people who provided something in return. He had convinced those who were asking for food that they had to contribute in some way, so he challenged them to restore the water and sewage system. And Joshua (he decided 'Josh' was too immature for his lofty position) was determined to ensure that there would be no accounting of who contributed more or who received the most. *"All are equal in the eyes of the Lord"*. Unfortunately, people didn't always see things through the eyes of the Lord.

Yes, he was certain he had made the right decision. This must be what God wanted, or else why would he have learned of the benefits of Socialism in college? Capitalism was a failed system that pitted brother against brother. This recent tragic turn of events that destroyed the fruits of Capitalism was God's way of giving humanity a chance to start over with a better plan. He was sure of it.

At least he had been sure until Mike and Liv showed up.

Joshua was troubled by his own actions. When Mike asked for help, it was Joshua's first instinct to turn him away! How could he justify that, when he had reprimanded the farmers for the same behavior? He had, in fact, only agreed to help after Sandra had pleaded on behalf of the strangers.

And, he reminded himself, there is more to this Mike character than a fellow human in need. Sandra remembered her earlier encounter and Joshua remembered how it had affected her. Mike hadn't challenged her belief in God, but he had convinced her to question the teachings of her Church! Joshua and Sandra were close friends at the time, so it was natural that she would come to him with her doubts – doubts she didn't dare share with the Elders. Joshua had counseled her then, and he had to protect his flock from such talk now.

Although Mike had tried to shirk his duty regarding Liv, he had ultimately accepted it without too much argument. Joshua had convinced him easily, even while questioning his *own* motivation. If Joshua had offered Liv sanctuary, the farmers would have rebelled again. He'd had no choice but to shame Mike into taking her with him.

He wasn't proud of that. It was the main reason he hastily

gathered some food from his own pantry before riding to Mike's house. That was the main reason. The other reason was a calculated one. Joshua had been stung by Mike's remark about only being willing to help members of his own Church. The magnanimous gesture was designed to show Mike how compassionate the Church was. But it failed! Mike had accepted the gift graciously but almost casually, returning the gesture by cooking a meal for all of them from his own meager supplies. All of this only served to increase Sandra's respect for the man. Joshua had been out-done.

Joshua had a gnawing feeling Mike would be his nemesis. They were from different worlds, and saw things differently. If only he hadn't shown up at the Church! But he was here now, and not likely to go away. That was when Joshua had the inspiration to ask for Mike's help with the water problem. He would have to put him in a subservient position where he could be controlled.

As he and Sandra rode back to her house, Joshua smiled while Sandra gushed about "what a nice man Mike was". He wasn't really listening to her. He was smiling as he recalled another quote he'd read:

"Keep your friends close and your enemies closer".

Chapter 7 – Liv

The sun was shining in his eyes. Mike woke slowly from a dream he wasn't quite ready to end, the lyrics of an old song tip-toeing through his half-awake brain. 'Life is but a dream'. Well, life was getting interesting, so the dream would have to wait until the next time he slept. Today he would meet Jonathon and find out if they had any reasonable hope of getting the water back on.

He thought about the possibilities as he attempted to get a little cleaner with his make-shift shower. Once dressed, he and Plato started down the stairs when Mike remembered he didn't live alone anymore. What was he going to do about Liv? He didn't want her following him everywhere, but could he trust her alone in his house? As soon as that thought flashed through his mind, he realized how paranoid it sounded. She didn't really seem to be a threat.

The Bishop, on the other hand, could be a potential adversary. That wasn't paranoia, it was reasonable caution. If he had made an enemy, it might be wise to try to make Liv an ally.

He climbed the stairs again and knocked on her door. "Liv, it's morning. Are you awake?" He waited, but there was no reply. The door was locked, and he didn't want to break it down, but what if she was dead? "Liv, are you okay?"

"Yes, I'm sorry. I was sound asleep. I'm getting up now. Wait just a minute while I get dressed." Relieved, Mike waited until she unlocked the door. "That was the best night's sleep I've had in a long time!"

"Glad to hear it. You deserved it after what you've been

through. Do you want a shower?"

"Thanks, but I don't want to impose on you anymore. I should probably just leave."

Mike was partly relieved to hear that, but the better part of him knew he should offer to let her stay longer. "Don't be silly. You didn't eat much last night. You must be starving. Come downstairs and have some breakfast, and we'll talk a little". After letting Plato out for his morning run, Mike explained "Sandra said you'd have trouble with solid foods for awhile, so try some of what I have for breakfast. It's nutritious and easy to digest. Just sit down and sip it slowly".

They sat quietly as Mike gathered his thoughts. He really didn't want her to leave, but he wasn't sure *why*. He'd been single for a lot of years and had been quite content to stay that way, but he had been lonely these last few weeks. It would be nice to have someone to talk with, even if the relationship remained platonic. In fact, he was pretty sure he only wanted a platonic relationship. Friendships often outlasted love affairs. He thought of the friends he'd had before and how, like his family, he had no idea if any of them were still alive. Mike wanted to explain all of this to Liv, but without sounding needy.

"Liv, I appreciate that you don't want to be an imposition but I'm going to be blunt. You don't really have anywhere to go! I don't know what the future will be like – I've given up making long-range plans - but for now, I think you should stay here. I've got a meeting scheduled with some folks who are working on getting the water and sewage systems working again. I aim to meet as many survivors as I can, and to try to find a way we can help each other out. Maybe we can find some work for you. Then, once you are self-sufficient, you can leave if you want. So, tell me a little more about yourself. What did you do before the blackout?"

She took a deep breath and gazed out at the trees, gently dancing in the breeze. "So, I suppose now is as good a time as any to review my life and lament the mistakes I made. Okay, here is the abridged version of Liv's life. While in high school, I learned I was never going to have children. From that moment, I decided to choose a career and be the best I could be at it. I studied hard and got my Law degree. After I had established myself as a successful Attorney, I met Mike. He was adorable. We married. I didn't care that I had to support him. I really loved him. Now, he's gone. My parents passed away years ago and I have no siblings. All I have to show for my lifetime of efforts is a Law practice, and I don't think the people who have survived will have much need for a lawyer. Life is funny, isn't it? I have always been self-sufficient. But now..."

Mike thought it would be rude to tell Liv he agreed with Shakespeare's opinion of lawyers. Instead, he tried to be more optimistic. "Without a court system, people are going to need another means of settling disputes. Maybe you could be a mediator, assuming we can get people to agree to arbitration."

That actually seemed to give Liv some hope. "Yes, that's a good idea. People may also need contracts written, and I could even offer Notary service. And who says there isn't a need for courts? I could be a judge."

"Whoa! Slow down, girl. Next thing, you'll be running for President!"

Liv laughed. It was a sound Mike thought he would like to hear often, but this wasn't the time to entertain fanciful thoughts. "For now, though, we should drive to your house and pick up some of your things. You look better in my jeans than I do, but you'd probably feel better in your own clothes".

She stopped laughing and turned pale. What had he said? Oh, of course. Her dead husband was at her house. "Listen, I know it won't be easy but we really need to do this. I'll be with you. We'll just go inside, get a few things and be back here in no time".

"You said you had a meeting".

"That's okay, it can wait. You're more important to me". *Oops! He didn't mean to say that. Until he heard the words spill out of his mouth, he hadn't realized how true it was. How would she take that? She hadn't reacted much at all. Maybe she didn't take it seriously, but Mike was going to have to give this revelation some serious thought. What was he getting himself into? There'd be time to think about that later. Right now, they needed to get her settled so he could meet Jonathan.*

After explaining to Plato that he needed to stay home and guard the house, Mike and Liv drove to her house. It was a large home. Mike's house was nice, but this was much nicer. She wasn't exaggerating when she said she had been successful. Would she be happy living with Mike? He had to stop these idle thoughts. They weren't getting married! She was just staying with him until she was back on her feet. Mike wished *that* thought didn't sadden him as much as it did.

Liv had selected a lot of clothes and what little food she had left in her house. Mike was grateful for that. At least she was contributing what she could to their mutual survival. It took a few trips up the stairs to bring her wardrobe to her new room, but as soon as the last load was deposited, Liv said "Thanks. Now give a lady a little privacy so she can put herself together. Don't you have a meeting to go to?"

He really didn't want to go. This was the happiest he had been in a long time, but he did have a meeting to go to, so he left - reluctantly. Plato was also reluctant to stay behind, but he was warming up to Liv. He wouldn't be alone today like he usually was when Mike went to work. Well, at least someone was happy with this new situation.

Chapter 8 – Water

The water treatment plant was about five miles away. Mike checked the gas gauge, but there was plenty of fuel left. At some point, that would be a problem. Would he have to get a horse? Where the heck would he keep a horse? He didn't look forward to losing his mobility.

There were no cars in the lot, but a lot of bicycles. That was his first clue that the people he was about to meet would be younger than he was. He hadn't even owned a bike in a very long time, let alone rode one. A lot of people rode to stay in shape, but he didn't have a weight problem, and he just didn't see the point in exerting himself if he didn't have to. Well, when the gas runs out he'd have to get a bicycle. That sounded more practical than a horse.

There were quite a few men milling around. No women. It was apparently a good thing Mike didn't bring Liv with him. But, while there were many men here, it didn't look like they knew what they were doing. He could only hope Jonathon knew more than these people did. Someone directed him to Jonathon, who looked to be about forty. He was studying some blueprints. They looked old, and Mike wondered if they were up to date. The newer stuff was probably on computers, and there didn't seem to be any power to run them.

Mike introduced himself and started to explain why he was there, but Jonathon cut him off. "Joshua told me to expect you. Glad you're here. We could use your expertise".

"I'm not an expert. And who is Joshua? Oh, you must mean the Bishop! He didn't tell me his name."

"Well, he told me you were a mechanical engineer."

"Ha-ha. Well, I was a draftsman a long, long time ago. I see you have some old schematics. They look as old as the stuff I used to work with, so at least I'll be able to read them. Are you sure they're accurate? A lot may have changed since these were drawn".

"Yeah, a lot has changed, but we need to rework this plant to operate the way it did before all this automation occurred. We can't generate enough power to run a modern plant, so we're trying to replace a lot of the equipment with older, mechanical stuff. That's why we dug up these old drawings".

"That makes sense! Well, let's see what you've got here". Jonathon and Mike spent the next several hours discussing what *would* work, what *might* work and what they would need to find or manufacture in order to have any hope of making *anything* work. They were a long way from turning on the water, but it was a start. And Mike was happy to be busy again.

They were still engrossed in their conversation when the Bishop – "Joshua" – arrived with lunch for everyone. To Mike, Joshua said "You came. Good. Are you making any progress?"

"I think we're making some headway, but there will be a lot of work ahead before we see any results. I'm glad you're here, though. There is something I want to discuss with both of you, but let's eat while we talk. I'm starving!"

They found an office where they could talk privately and Mike continued. "I don't really know that much about water treatment plants, but I know something about human nature. When the water pressure started dropping I'd venture a guess that most everyone opened their faucets to capture as much water as they could. I know I did". They both agreed that was likely.

Mike continued, "Then - and here's where the human nature part comes in - a lot of people panicked when the water stopped flowing. It's irrational, but I imagine a lot of people ran to other rooms and opened *those* faucets. And, because nothing was coming out, a lot of people didn't bother to close the faucets! Before we can turn on the water, assuming we can get the pressure up enough to do that, we are going to have to pay a visit to every building in town. Otherwise, water is going to spew out of a lot of open faucets and the pressure is going to drop like a rock".

The two men stared in silence. Jonathon finally spoke. "You're right. And not just homes, but businesses and any sprinklers that were on when the power went out, too. The timers will still be in the 'on' position, so the water will be on, too".

Joshua was shaking his head. "We can't close every faucet in every house! No one will want to go into empty houses. Who knows what we'll find."

"I thought about that before I brought this up. We don't have to go into the houses. We just need to turn off the water at every meter. That's still a lot of work. We'll need the assistance of every able-bodied person you can muster, Joshua, but it has to be done if we are going to succeed". Mike waited until Joshua agreed and thought, "Good, now I'm giving the orders and Joshua is working for me". Then he introduced the next part of his plan.

"It's not as bad as it sounds. This gives us a great opportunity to conduct a census of sorts. You only know of the people in your Church, but there may be others who survived. Until yesterday, you didn't know about me – or Liv. And anyone who did survive this long must be resourceful. Some of them may have skills we don't have. If we can offer them water, we'll be in a good bargaining position to recruit their help".

Jonathon was enthusiastic. He wanted to get as much help as he could. Although Joshua didn't say anything, it was apparent he was not as pleased with the idea. That was understandable. He was in charge of all these people because they accepted his authority, but he wouldn't find it so easy to control outsiders. Mike wasn't sure *he* would be able to, either, but it would be his only chance to tilt the balance of power.

Joshua left them after promising to schedule a Ward meeting for Saturday, at which time Jonathon would have the opportunity to explain what was needed. At first, Mike was offended that he would not have the opportunity to address the group, but it was probably better that they heard it from one of their own. Jonathon was on board with Mike's ideas. Things would go more smoothly this way.

They spent the afternoon pouring over the schematics and making plans. Mike would have continued into the night, but Jonathon called an end to it. Everyone wanted to get home before dark. They agreed to meet the next morning, and all the men headed home to their families. Mike just headed home.

It was still light when he pulled into the garage. Mike was tired. He had been enthusiastic and full of energy all the while they were working on the water problem, but now he was aware of how that activity – no matter how enjoyable – had worn him out. He had been living a sedentary lifestyle until yesterday which allowed him to sustain himself on his morning nutritional drink and one meal mid-afternoon. If he kept up this pace, he was going to have to eat more. And there wasn't much food left, especially with a second mouth to feed. Liv! What was he going to do about Liv?

As soon as he unlocked the door to the house, Liv shouted "Mike, is that you? You're home!" And she threw her arms around him. Mike was stunned. This wasn't what he expected, and he was a bit troubled by how good it felt. This was not how platonic friends acted – or felt.

Before he could react, she pulled away and attempted to apologize. "I'm sorry, I didn't mean…You said you were going to meet a lot of strangers and I thought about how dangerous that might be, and you were gone so long, and…I was afraid you might not come back". The apology was genuine. Liv hated feeling dependent. It seemed silly to become attached to someone she hardly knew. She thought to herself *Get a grip, girl!*

Liv started over. "I'm sorry. The last couple of days have been so out of the ordinary. I let my imagination run away with me". He could understand that. He had certainly succumbed to his share of flights of fancy lately. Mostly, about her.

It seemed like a good time to change the subject, so he said "Did you eat anything while I was gone?"

"Yes. Yes, I nuked the leftovers from last night's dinner. It was delicious! Have you had anything to eat?"

"Yes, Joshua – that's the Bishop's name – he brought us lunch."

He told her most of what had occurred that day, leaving out his private thoughts on the power struggle between himself and the Bishop.

Then he added, "You look nice". She was wearing a tailored dress and had expertly applied just the right amount of makeup. Mike had noticed all of that as soon as he walked in, but hadn't been sure if he should comment on it. *Damn* she looked good! He could see that the compliment had been appreciated, but it was time to change the subject again.

"So, what have you done all day?"

"Oh, I just relaxed and recuperated – when I wasn't worrying obsessively over you". She giggled, as if to dismiss it as a joke, but Mike sensed she was serious. "You know. I've always believed you can tell a lot about a man by the books he's read, but you have a pretty extensive library. There are Sci-Fi books, which tell me you have an imagination, and some serious real science books that say you are grounded in reality. You have the King James Bible, but you also have the Book of Mormon, the I Ch'ing and several books by the Dalai Lama – and by Richard Bach! Have you read all of them?"

"Most of them. Some of them several times. I try to keep an open mind. There are usually more than two sides to every argument. People are too willing to choose one of the two loudest – left or right, Christian or Atheist, Socialism or Capitalism. The truth is somewhere in between. Once you understand all the variations that exist, you'll find that both extremes miss the mark. It would be a better world if more people sought the truth instead of choosing sides".

They passed the evening in philosophical discussions, not

always agreeing, but challenging each other to defend a position or rethink it. It had been a good day for Mike, and an even better evening. Was it less than forty-eight hours ago that he had wondered if surviving was worth the effort? Now he knew it was.

The conversation had been invigorating, but they were both yawning now. It was time to go to bed. Time for another awkward moment! Neither said anything, but at the top of the stairs Liv said good night as she walked into 'her' room and closed the door behind her. Well, that was settled. Maybe they *could* be just friends.

Chapter 9 – The New Normal

During the next three days, Mike's life was a little more normal. He got up every morning, shaved, got dressed and went to work. Plato was used to being left alone, but now he had Liv for company – and Liv had a new friend.

Mike and Jonathon worked well together, and they were really making progress. Seeing that progress, the other men were more willing to make an effort to help when they were asked. When Mike had first arrived, most of them were content to sit around playing cards while they waited for Joshua to bring them lunch. It reminded Mike of what union auto workers used to do when they were furloughed but still paid as long as they showed up, because their contract guaranteed them full pay - even if they weren't needed.

Since Mike was part of the so-called work force here at the plant, he was entitled to lunch with the rest of them. Unlike most of them, he actually earned it! Mike had noticed that the men filled their bellies and then filled their lunch buckets, presumably to bring food home for their families. Mike only took what he could consume for lunch. But despite the free meal each day, the food supply at home was dwindling with Liv there. He didn't begrudge her the food. He really enjoyed her company and their talks every evening after dinner. But he also knew they couldn't continue this way forever.

That's what made what happened on Friday afternoon so difficult.

Joshua always arrived with lunch, received a briefing from Mike and Jonathon and left. Today, he returned just before quitting time with large quantities of food meant to feed the men and their families over the weekend. Mike was torn between his stubborn pride and his knowledge that he and Liv really needed help. His pride won. Mike decided he'd have to 'go shopping' for more canned goods over the weekend. He and Liv were not going to become charity cases like so many of the Church members!

There was good news, too. Joshua reminded Jonathon of the meeting he had scheduled for Saturday, then turned to Mike and said "You'll be there too, of course. You can help explain what needs to be done. After all, it was your idea".

"Absolutely, just tell me when and where? Oh, and can I bring Liv along? She would probably like to get out of the house and meet some of the women. Will they be there?"

"Yes, everyone is coming to the meeting. Liv is welcome to come. Sandra will be pleased to see her again, and I'm sure she'll introduce her around. We'll see you both at 10AM at the Church".

As soon as Mike got home, he told Liv the news. "Hey, we've been invited to the social event of the season!"

"Oh, no, I was afraid this would happen. Don't tell me you've joined the Church!"

"Ha-ha. That's not going to happen. But we *are* going to the church". He explained the purpose of the meeting, and then he added "You've been stuck in this little house for almost a week. You must be dying to get out and talk to someone besides me".

"First, I haven't been stuck. I could leave anytime I wanted, if I was so inclined. Second, this house is not so little. Third –"

Mike interrupted her: "You really are a lawyer, aren't you? Hold your closing arguments, Counselor. I concede! But seriously, if you don't want to go, you don't have to. I'd like you to, though".

"I'd like to. And I like that you'd like me to. It's a date!"

Suddenly, Mike felt as nervous as he had on his *first* date!

Chapter 10 – The Mormons

Saturday morning looked like the dawn of another beautiful day. Mike awoke early, even though he had nowhere to go until 9:30. He had wanted to sleep in, but sleep doesn't come easily when you are worried. Today would be his first chance to meet with the farmers who supplied his lunches. He had only heard about them from the men at the plant, and they didn't have many kind words for their benefactors. Joshua tried to give the impression that everyone in the church was one big happy family, but over the past three days Mike had learned otherwise.

From what he gathered, the founding families had always resented the city folk that occupied the new homes – homes like his – that had displaced so many family farms. Of course, all this new construction couldn't have happened if some of the farmers hadn't been willing to sell their land to developers, but the remaining farmers blamed the new arrivals instead of placing the blame on their own kind that sold out. Relations were already strained, but now that the farmers were expected to feed everyone, tensions had heightened. If they didn't like their new neighbors even though they shared the same religion, what were they going to think of him!

Of course, it might not be as bad as he had been led to believe. The men he had met had been successful businessmen and professionals before the blackout. They had lost much more than the farmers. Worse than that, they had probably considered themselves superior to their country cousins, but now found themselves completely dependent upon them for what must seem like charity. Some of their talk could be the result of wounded pride. Mike couldn't ignore the similarity between their situation and Liv's. Did she resent him as much as the men at the plant resented those who fed them?

When Liv joined him for breakfast, Mike told her all he knew about the conflict. She would need to know what she was walking into this morning. Her reaction wasn't what he expected.

"Oh, great, now I don't know what to wear!"

"Huh?"

"If I dress professionally, the farmer's wives will resent me. If I wear jeans, the city wives will shun me. You really don't know what a problem you've handed me!"

"Here's a thought. Be yourself. How long have you lived in this town? You must already know some of these people. And that means you can't pretend to be someone you're not."

"Good point. Tell me some of their names."

"I only know a few of them by name, and only by their first names. I doubt if that will help". Mike was always terrible at remembering names, but he didn't want to admit it to Liv. Why did he care so much what she thought of him?

"Besides, as an attorney you are probably accustomed to dealing with people from all walks of life. Be yourself and you'll be in a better position than I am. You're not the one trying to convince them to do something they're not gonna want to do."

Actually, Mike was quite good at getting people to do things they didn't originally want to do. He could be very persuasive, but only in a one-on-one situation. He hated public speaking because you can't read the body language of a whole room full of people at once. Joshua had said he wanted Jonathon to explain what they were doing, and Mike was beginning to think that was really for the best. He'd let Jonathon take the lead, and then offer to answer individual questions as they came up. He could deal with individuals...but only if they managed to get to the meeting.

Liv had gone upstairs to dress at least a half-hour ago. What was taking so long? Mike remembered how often he had asked that question while waiting for his wife. "Why do men always have to wait for their wives?" Plato gave no reply. Smart dog. *Oh, great, now I'm thinking of Liv as my wife!*

"Liv, are you almost ready? We have to go soon".

"I'm ready. Do I look okay?" She wore a tailored gray pin-striped pant suit and medium height heels. She had put her hair up, which showed a small pair of earrings that matched her necklace. Subtle elegance was the term that came to Mike's mind.

"You look much better than okay".

On the short drive to the church, Mike confessed to being "a little nervous". He didn't like to appear weak, but he really wanted some moral support from her. She didn't disappoint.

"Mike, you are both articulate and knowledgeable. The best advice I can give you is something I was told recently. Be yourself".

There were more cars in the church parking lot than bicycles. Apparently, people had been rationing their gas for use when they had to travel as a family, and they had brought their entire families to hear the news about the water.

As soon as they entered the church, Sandra rushed up. "Hi Liv, you look wonderful! Come with me, and I'll introduce you to some of the women your age." Of course, she regretted those words as soon as she uttered them. Sandra was a kind, gentle soul but no one would accuse her of being pretentious. She couldn't seem to avoid saying exactly what she was thinking, even when those thoughts would be better kept to herself.

"I mean, you wouldn't want to spend your time with someone like me – I'm young enough to be your daughter." That didn't sound any better. Rather than dig the hole any deeper, she quickly introduced Liv to a woman nearby.

"Marcie Harmon may I introduce Liv...I'm sorry, I don't know your last name!"

"It's Wilson. Olivia Wilson. Pleased to meet you, Marcie. Are you any relation to John Harmon?"

"Yes, that's my husband. Have we met?"

"No, but I represented his firm in a merger a few years ago". Liv was, if not among friends, at least in her element. Mike wasn't as fortunate. He really only knew two men there - Jonathon and Joshua - and he was only comfortable in the company of one of them.

Joshua was calling the meeting to order, or trying to. It was a few minutes before all the private conversations wound down and he had everyone's attention.

"As you know, we are here to learn of the progress our brothers have made in getting the water flowing again. We have enlisted the expert assistance of someone most of you haven't met. Mike, stand up so everyone will know you". Mike stood, and everyone applauded even though they had no idea what news he was going to give them. They were hopeful, and that was enough for now.

Joshua nodded to Jonathon and continued: "You all know Jonathon. Let's have him tell us what has been happening at the plant". Jonathon approached the podium and Mike was grateful for the opportunity to sit down.

Jonathon proceeded to explain in great detail every step they had taken. From the blank gazes on the faces of everyone in the room, Mike could see Jonathon – a knowledgeable engineer – was even less adept at public speaking than Mike was. He was talking in terms too technical for his audience. That's not the way to get their cooperation. Now, after being reluctant to address this crowd, Mike couldn't wait for his turn. When Jonathon reached the point in his long narrative where it was time to tell them what *they* were going to have to do, Mike stepped up and took the microphone.

"Jonathon has explained the details, so let me just take a moment to sum it up. We believe we've solved the technical problems facing us, but there is one problem we can't solve without your help. Before we can turn on the water, all the meters outside of all the buildings that aren't occupied have to be turned off. If not, precious water will spill out of open faucets and drain the pressure we have been working to restore. We can't complete this project without your assistance, and Joshua – your Bishop – has assured me that you are all anxious to be a part of this historic moment when our lives get a little closer to normal".

For the second time today, the audience applauded. This time they had good reason. He had given them some good news and also offered them the opportunity to be heroes. Mike unrolled a map of the town. He had divided the town up into zones, with a big number on each one. The he told them what he would do, before asking them to do their part.

"I live in this zone, so I will take responsibility for shutting the meters here. I need volunteers for each of the other zones. Let's start with this one. Who lives in or near this zone?"

One by one, people responded until commitments had been made for each zone. Once he had their cooperation, it was time to give them the down-side of this venture.

"Now, we all want to be safe. I don't think you will encounter anyone you don't already know, but if there are any survivors out there that we don't know about, this will be a good opportunity to explain what we're doing and recruit their help! Remember, you don't have to go inside any buildings, but if someone sees you near their house they are probably going to want to know what you're doing. It's not likely you'll find anyone, but no one should go out alone, and it would be a good idea if each team had a weapon – just in case".

There was some grumbling. That was to be expected. He'd have to smooth this over a bit more, but it was better they knew the possible dangers now and prepared for them.

"Now, I don't think anyone will be violent if you explain that you're trying to provide them with water! But it would be wise to be armed. Having a weapon should keep someone from shooting first and asking questions later. You just need a few minutes to tell them why you're there, and they'll be on your side. And that's only if you even encounter anyone, which isn't very likely."

Once the business portion of the meeting had been completed, the private conversations that had been reluctantly terminated now resumed. No one seemed anxious to go home. Mike had been right. This really was the social event of the season! He had never liked cocktail parties, not that there were any cocktails being served at *this* party, but Liv seemed to be enjoying it.

Most people were enthusiastic about the chance of having running water again, and many of them wanted to shake his hand. He did his best to smile and mingle, for Liv's sake, but he glanced in her direction often, in the hopes of seeing any indication that she might be ready to leave. It was going to be a long afternoon.

At one point, Joshua took Mike aside. "It seems you have taken good care of Liv. She certainly looks healthier and happier than she did the night we met."

"Yes, she has recovered considerably. I don't think she is ready to go out on her own yet, though. We'll just take things a day at a time".

"Fine, fine. I commend you for your behavior and also for how well prepared you must have been before this catastrophe. I'm sure, though, you're food supplies must be dwindling since you were not prepared to feed two people, and I've noticed you haven't taken any food home with you. Mike, you are performing a valuable service for our community, and food is the only way we have to repay you. I wish you would reconsider, if not for yourself, then for Liv".

Joshua was giving Mike a way to accept this charitable gift while saving face. Mike had to admit, Joshua would make a great salesman – or politician. Well, he'd better accept now while he could still do so with his dignity intact.

"As long as we consider it as wages for services rendered, I accept".

Apparently, Joshua was confident in his own abilities. He had already prepared a large crate which he discretely helped load into the trunk of Mike's car. Mike's pride had taken a hit, but he figured it was okay to lose one battle if doing so meant living to fight another day. He was already hatching a plan for a future where charity would not be the normal way to acquire food.

Chapter 11 – Confession

On the way home, Mike had to explain why there was an abundance of fresh food in the trunk. He was still not comfortable with his decision to accept it, but if he hadn't they would not survive much longer. That reality hadn't made the decision more palatable. Mike was proud, but he was a realist. Now, he had to find a way to put a positive spin on what he considered 'selling out'.

"The meeting turned out better than I'd hoped. People have accepted the challenge, and there is a real good chance we will get the water flowing – and the toilets flushing. What was your take on the mood in the room, Liv? You were more able to mingle than I was."

"It turns out I *do* know some of the town's people, but I had never met any of the farmers. The ones I met tonight were polite but cool. I got the impression the two sides were going to cooperate for now, but the tension between them won't be going away any time soon. It's a battle between the producers who feel they are being taken advantage of, and the takers who are more resentful than grateful for what they receive. I'm not sure I understand the attitude of the latter, but I can sympathize with the former. Ironically, I find myself siding with the people who consider me the enemy!"

"Well, maybe I can help you understand what the 'takers' are feeling, since I just became one of them. Joshua has been offering me food since I started helping at the plant. I've taken only what I needed to eat for lunch, but I've refused to take food home like everyone else does...until tonight. We have a 'care package' in the trunk. He put it diplomatically, saying that I've earned it and that food is the only way they have of paying me, but it still doesn't sit well with me. I keep thinking of all the TV ads the government used to run to convince people they were entitled to food stamps. Those ads worked. The number of people on government subsistence nearly doubled in a year! I guess it's easy for a lot of people to take what's offered and rationalize it. Or maybe most people struggle with the decision like I am. I really don't know. But I think the folks in this town, who are used to being self-reliant, are struggling the same way I am."

"Hmm..."

"That's it? That's all you've got to say?"

"Look, Mike, I've been surviving on your kindness for awhile now and I am grateful! I can't tell you how grateful, but I'm not resentful. That's the part I don't understand. Remember, I was also self-sufficient. Circumstances beyond my control have changed that. I hope the situation is temporary, but for now I don't see that I've had a choice. Why should I blame anyone? It's not anyone's fault, especially not yours. Gratitude is understandable. Resentment is not."

"Yeah, maybe resentment on the part of one side is uncalled for, but you said you understood why the farmers are resentful, right? They are being asked to support a lot of people who haven't done anything in return. It probably doesn't help that the farmers were already unhappy with all these city folks like us who turned their quiet little rural town into a sea of red-tile roofs."

"Yes, the resentment on their part started before the blackout, and it's not unfounded. We did destroy their utopian existence, and if we weren't here now, they would have no problem growing enough food for just themselves. I *do* feel for them, because their situation *is* someone else's fault."

Suddenly, her expression changed. "Oh, I'm so stupid! It just dawned on me. If I weren't here, your food supply would have lasted a lot longer. You had to take what Joshua offered...*for me!* Mike, I'm so sorry! This is my fault, and you have every right to be resentful."

"NO! That's not what I meant! Liv, I..." They were home. This would have to wait. Mike had a lot of explaining to do, and he couldn't see how he could do that without telling her he loved her.

Neither spoke while they unloaded the crate. When everything had been put away, Liv started up the stairs. "It's been quite a day and I'm tired. Good night."

"Please don't. I'm sure you're tired. So am I, but I don't want to leave things this way. Can we talk for a little bit?"

"I told you I'm sorry. I don't know what else I can say, Mike."

"You don't have to say anything. I don't have any right to ask this, but please listen. I have some explaining to do."

She hesitated, then walked into the study and sat down. "I don't understand. You don't owe me an explanation, but I'll listen if that's what you want me to do."

Mike took a deep breath and began. He was not accustomed to speaking before he knew what he was going to say, but tonight he couldn't take the time to think first. He would have to be open and honest with her, and maybe for the first time he'd also be honest with himself.

"I have worked for most of my life. To make a living it was necessary to interact with others. I didn't enjoy it. I loved my wife and my children, but half the time I resented the time I had to spend with *them* on a daily basis. I actually looked forward to the day when I might be able to retire and enjoy the solitude I had always craved. I'm not proud of that, but it is how I have always felt." That wasn't easy to admit, but he couldn't stop now.

"After the blackout, I was actually relieved. I didn't have to go to work anymore. I wouldn't have to deal with co-workers or bosses. My neighbors were all leaving. I was finally going to be alone. But, after four weeks with no company but Plato, I thought I was going to lose my mind! Plato is a good dog but not a very good conversationalist. The second night you were here, we talked for hours and I felt more alive than I've felt in...maybe ever! I realized that it wasn't having people around that bothered me - it was having the *wrong* people around. I have enjoyed every minute we have spent together and I want to spend the rest of my life with you."

She was about to speak, but Mike wasn't finished.

"Please don't say anything yet. I don't have any right to expect you to feel the way I do, although I can hope you do. But I don't want to know yet! You said you are here because circumstances left you no choice. I understand that. And I don't resent you at all, because you have given me more than a little food could repay, even if you didn't mean to. Our circumstances *will* change, and you *will* have a choice someday. When that happens, I hope you'll stay because you want to, but if you decide to leave I won't try to stop you. You're not in a position to decide now, so don't say anything. Now you know how I feel about you. Someday I'll learn how you feel about me, but I'll wait until you have no strings holding you back from being honest. *Now* let's go to bed."

Chapter 12 – Seeds of Commerce

Sunday morning. How Mike used to relish Sundays! It was the one day of the week he could sleep in with no guilt. But he wasn't sleeping in this morning. In fact, he hadn't slept much all night. What had he been thinking, blurting out all that emotional crap! He had acted like a school kid with his first crush. Even worse, he *felt* like a school kid in love. He was staying in bed this morning, but not for pleasure. He didn't want to face Liv.

Well, he couldn't hide in bed all day. Especially since Plato, who was usually very patient, was getting a little antsy. He'd grab a quick breakfast and go out. He had to turn off the water mains in front of his neighbors houses. That would keep him busy and away from home – away from Liv – for most of the day. He showered and got dressed without shaving because "It's Sunday, damn it. That's got to mean something, doesn't it Plato?"

When Mike and Plato reached the kitchen, Liv was already there…cooking! "Good morning! Do you like omelets? I couldn't pass up the chance to use these fresh eggs and veggies!"

He loved omelets! There was no way he was going to turn down this feast. So she was going to be cool and act like nothing happened? Good. That would work. But after breakfast he would still go out, before things got weird.

"This is delicious. I didn't know you could cook."

"I didn't want to interfere with your routine before, but I want to be…useful."

Too late, things were already weird. Why didn't he keep his

mouth shut last night? We can't undo what's been done, but we can learn from our mistakes. So, since it's impolite to talk with your mouth full, he would make sure he kept his mouth too full to talk until the meal was over.

"That was great, thanks. I'm going to get started on shutting the water mains."

"Give me a minute to get dressed."

"What?"

"I can't go out dressed like this, so give me a minute."

"You don't have to come."

"Yesterday you said no one should go out alone, that it wouldn't be safe. You were right, so I'm coming with you, unless you have another partner picked out." She smiled. He really liked her smile.

Using one of the special wrenches Jonathon had passed out after the meeting, Mike turned the valves off with little effort. While Mike worked and Plato supervised, Liv watched the windows of each house for any signs of life. Mike was pretty certain there wouldn't be any. If there were any other survivors here in his own neighborhood, he would have heard something by now. She didn't need to be there, but even though neither of them had spoken since breakfast, he was glad she had come along.

After about an hour, the routine was getting boring and Mike broke the silence. "Liv, there is something else you might be able to help me with. I get the impression that Joshua would be content if this town remained as a simple, agrarian society.

Although he's been college educated and done some traveling, he was raised here. He's a farm boy at heart. I'm anxious to get the water back on so we can live a more citified life, but Joshua's motivation is to provide more water for irrigation. He's only thinking about the farmers. We need to help the others find a way to build a meaningful life for themselves – and for us."

"Okay, you've got my attention, but how do you propose to do that and how can I help?"

"You said you know some of the city folk here. Would you make a list of everyone you know or that you know anything about? You know, what they did before. I want to sort of take an inventory of the skills we might have at our disposal. When I'm back at the plant tomorrow, I'll try to talk to some of them privately. I want to see if I can help people set up businesses. If they can offer products or services the farmers might want, they could *buy* food instead of having to wait for someone to give it to them. That should go a long way toward relieving the tension between them. We'll have to set up some sort of barter system, since dollars are worthless."

"Hmm, that sounds interesting. You said before that you thought there might be a need for a mediator. You must have had this in mind for some time."

"Yeah, but I figured we needed to get them to cooperate on this water project first. If we couldn't accomplish that, none of my other ideas would have a chance of working. I'm a believer in Laissez Faire Capitalism. Joshua seems to lean more toward Marxist Socialism. I'm going to have to tread carefully, but I can't do nothing!"

"If you don't mind some free legal advice, a barter system can be messy. There would definitely be a need for a mediator, but I'm afraid most of the disputes would be difficult to resolve. How do you determine the right price for various things? Like…how many chickens should it take to buy a horse?"

"Ha-ha. And how many does it take to replace a light bulb? Seriously, I get it, but in a free market economy, there is one simple rule: The right price is what the buyer is willing to pay and the seller is willing to take. That's how commerce was conducted for eons. We have lost the willingness to haggle over price. We'll have to teach people to do that. No longer will products have price tags on them that we just have to pay. The seller shouldn't set the price by himself. It takes the cooperation of both buyer and seller to find an agreeable price. That price will have a lot to do with how much demand there is for a product and how many of them are available. That's how supply and demand works."

Mike hadn't planned on giving a lecture, but this was a topic important to him, and Liv seemed open to listening so he continued.

"That's also how employment should be dealt with. It's a contract between employer and employee, right? If no one is willing to work for the wages the employer offers, he has to raise the wage. The employer who offers the highest wages gets to pick his employees, but if an employee asks for too much, the employer can say 'no, I can't afford that much', or 'no, you're not worth that much'. Without labor unions guaranteeing everyone the same wage, people will earn what they're worth. The more skills an employee has, the higher the wages he'll be offered. That's supply and demand in action, too. I'll bet you didn't work for minimum wage! Neither did plumbers, doctors, auto mechanics…"

"Of course I didn't" Liv replied. It cost me a lot of money and time to gain my skills, and my fees reflected that. Unskilled laborers don't have to train for their jobs, so they get minimum wage."

"But minimum wage is another thing that was wrong with our society, Liv. It only makes sense from the perspective of the employee because there is some minimum income necessary to support a life, but there are no minimum values for skills. 'Unskilled' means anyone could do it. Not that everyone would *want* to do it, but anyone *could* because it requires no skill. From the employer's perspective that means there are a whole lot more potential employees for an unskilled position, and when supply exceeds demand the price should go down. We've seen automation replace a lot of those positions because the employer couldn't afford to pay minimum wage for the work that is being done. Sometimes the work accomplished wasn't worth the price he had to pay."

"So you're saying if there was no minimum wage, more people would find work. But what good would that do them if they couldn't earn enough to live? What would you say to that person, Mike?"

"I'd tell that unskilled laborer to get some skills. What sort of person goes all through life without learning...*anything?* No one should be unskilled forever. Doctors work for next to nothing while they are interns. They do it because they are learning skills that will pay more, later. You probably worked as an unpaid intern, too, didn't you?"

It was this kind of discussion that kept Mike energized. Before they realized it, they had completed their task. Every house in the subdivision was disconnected from the town's water supply except Mike's.

When they returned home, Liv started listing the people she knew. She had wanted to be useful, and now she felt better knowing Mike needed her. If he had given her half a chance last night, she would have told him how much she cared for him. It was probably best that she didn't. He might not believe her - yet. Mike's idea of helping people set up businesses really appealed to her. If she could become self-sufficient again, Mike would have to realize that she was with him because she wanted to be, not because she had no choice.

Mike cooked dinner early because they hadn't had lunch and because she made breakfast. That seemed only fair, and he didn't want her to stop making that list. After dinner, he reviewed it with her and took some notes of his own. This town was going to have more to offer than fruits and vegetables! Tomorrow, he would start planting the seeds of ideas that, with proper nurturing, could produce a diverse crop of businesses.

"Liv, I was thinking about what you said about the problems with barter and I have an idea for a monetary system we could implement."

"I thought about it, too. Gold and other precious metals were used for centuries, but I don't know if anyone has any. And what about those who don't? I can't see how it would work. People who have gold would be rich without having done anything to earn it, while others would be poor until they sold something – probably food. Eventually, the person with the gold will have spent it all and will end up poor, while the farmers would get rich."

"Exactly. We need a new form of currency. But rather than revert to what worked in ancient times, let's think 21st century. In modern times, cash has been nearly replaced with digital money. So, why not have only digital credits? When a person buys something they are debited and the seller is credited. No actual money has to change hands."

"I must be getting stupid in my old age, but I don't get it. There aren't any banks."

"Think about how Visa made its money. They earned a small percentage of every transaction, just for keeping track of the credits and debits. They credited the merchant's bank account and debited the purchaser's bank account. We can do that without banks. We'll take a 4% fee for handling and recording each transaction and for settling any disputes that might arise. But since there is no actual cash, there's no need for actual banks. We'll be a virtual bank."

"Okay, that's a little clearer, but no one has any credits to start with. Why would anyone sell something to a buyer who has no money?"

"I said we'll be *like* a bank. Banks make loans. We will make loans to people who want to set up businesses. Most people take out a loan when starting a business, only unlike banks, we won't charge interest. The only fees will be the per transaction fees on every sale. Initially, the only people who will be able to buy and sell will be those who offer a product or service for sale. They'll all be members of a 'merchants club'. Every member will be a merchant and they'll also be consumers. And we will make money by putting them together and keeping them in business. Once a business is established, the merchant may want to hire help. The employees will earn credits and become consumers, too."

All the walking they had done was beginning to take its toll on both of them, and they were ready to put this day to bed. Plato had dozed off a few hours earlier. Mike said "Thanks for all your help today, Liv. And not just for the things you did, but also for the conversation."

"I enjoyed it, too. I think we make a good team. Is there anything I can do tomorrow while you're at the plant? I've got way too much time on my hands, and I want to get this going as much as you do."

"There is, actually. Some of the professionals on your list are women. Only the men go to the plant, so you'll need to talk to the women. But there aren't any phones, so you'll have to go to them. If you're serious about teaming up, why don't you drive me to work tomorrow, so you'll have the car?"

"Are you trusting me with your car?"

"Yeah, I'm also trusting you to pick me up at the end of the day. Should I be worried?"

"Ha-ha, well you did cook a nice dinner for me tonight, so I guess I owe you."

They were both looking forward to Monday. It was time to get some rest, so they climbed the stairs together. At the top, they both paused but, without saying a word, went to their own bedrooms.

Chapter 13 – Culture Shock

Mike woke early on Monday, anxious to begin his covert operation. His mind was racing as he showered and shaved. Was he moving too fast? What would Joshua do if he got wind of Mike's plans before they were ready to implement them? The men didn't talk with Joshua, but Jonathon did. Mike would have to be careful around Jonathon. He'd better tell Liv to avoid talking in front of any of the farmers' wives, too. *No, she's a lawyer, not a child. Don't insult her intelligence. She would understand the need for discretion without being told. They made a good team. She had actually said that last night!* He hoped she meant it.

Liv was up early, too. Good. They were certainly functioning as a team.

"I probably don't have to tell you this, but a lot of what we discussed should remain between the two of us for now. I don't want people arguing about the financial aspects before they've even considered what sort of business they might be able to create."

"You're right. You don't have to tell me. I'm an attorney, remember? Haven't you heard of attorney-client privilege? I would have been out of business pretty quickly if I blabbed all of my client's secrets!"

"Sorry. I'm just not used to this cloak-and-dagger stuff, but I can see the need for secrecy. I suppose you've been a party to plenty of this sort of thing."

"Well, I'm glad you are acquiring an appreciation for this 'stuff'. Maybe now you'll have a higher opinion of attorneys."

"I never said I had a low opinion of people in your profession!"

"You didn't have to." And she smiled. He couldn't get mad at her when she smiled.

As they headed toward the garage, Plato tried to join them. "Sorry, boy, you have to stay here and guard the house". Poor Plato. He hadn't been left alone much for over a month.

Mike drove them to the plant and then Liv slid behind the wheel. "This car is too big. Do I need a truck driver's license for this?"

"What did you drive, a Prius?"

"Oh, please! I have a 3-series BMW coupe."

"Well, after you pick me up at four, we'll go get your car. I have jumper cables in the trunk. Do you remember if it has any gas in it?"

"Oh, I don't know! But we'll find out. I'll be back at four o'clock."

He almost leaned in and kissed her. It seemed like the natural thing to do, but nothing was as it seemed these days. He settled for giving her what he hoped was a charming smile, and walked into the plant.

"Morning, Jonathon. How did it go?"

"What do you mean?"

"Liv and I turned off the water in our subdivision. How far did everyone else get?"

"Mike, yesterday was Sunday. We don't work on Sundays."

"Oh... It looks like everyone is here today. When are they going to find the time to shut the water valves?"

"Joshua assigned the young people to that task. I suppose they're doing it now. The farmers are working their fields, and he told us to keep working here."

Mike had to grit his teeth to keep from yelling 'With Joshua in charge, we'll be lucky if this ever gets done'. But Joshua *was* in charge of all these men and their families, and there was nothing Mike could do about that...yet. He'd have to find a way to talk to the people on his list. First he needed to make sure Jonathon was busy with...something, so he wouldn't interrupt.

"Okay, as long as it's getting done, I guess. Where are we on our project? Have you checked the valves on the south side this morning?"

Jonathon went off to inspect the valves as Mike suggested. That would take at least an hour. Mike looked around for his first 'interviewee'. His day was spent sending Jonathon on various missions that he hoped didn't sound too suspicious. Mike was able to talk with everyone he thought had some potential. Unfortunately, none of the 'applicants' lived up to his expectations. Dejected, he struggled to stay focused on the real work at hand until four o'clock rolled around.

Liv was waiting in the parking lot. As he got in on the passenger side she said "Hi, Honey, how was your day?" She was barely able to finish the sentence before she started giggling, and Mike couldn't avoid laughing. It was just what he needed to lighten his mood.

Still laughing, he said "Funny you should ask me that! My day was a disaster, how was yours?"

"What's wrong?" She wasn't laughing now. "What happened?"

"These men... I'm sure they enjoyed good paying positions with their respective firms, but they were just highly educated cogs in corporate wheels, incapable of making independent decisions and completely devoid of any entrepreneurial spirit. They wouldn't know how to run a business if their lives depended on it. Unfortunately, their lives *might* depend on it, but they don't even realize that. I hope you had better luck than I did."

"Not really. Most of these women have never had careers. They graduated from prestigious universities, but it seems they majored in finding a husband to support them. Their husbands were my clients, but I didn't socialize with them and never had any reason to get to know the wives. They all have children, but always relied on others to raise them while they shopped or stayed busy with charitable work. Not soup-kitchen charities, of course. No, they hosted dinners and solicited contributions from other equally vacuous socialites. Now they find themselves having to stay home and actually raise their own children. You will never find a more depressed group of women. I'm sure they'd all be on drugs if they had access to any."

"Right about now, I'd consider that, too - or at least a few stiff drinks! Do you want to get your car, or should we just go home?"

"I don't need the car, really. Let's go home."

They drove in silence. Mike was trying to think of some other way to move forward with his plan, and Liv seemed to recognize his need for quiet. They really were a good team.

Liv stopped the car in front of the garage. "This thing is a tank! You obviously like the car, so if you don't want it damaged it will probably be better if you park it. I swear it looks wider than the garage door."

"I have to put up with a grown woman who drives around in a kiddie-car. You're an adult. If you have to have a German status symbol you could at least get a 7-series."

They were both kidding, and they both enjoyed it. Things hadn't turned out well today, but as long as Liv was around, Mike thought life would be pretty good.

They prepared dinner together. Liv was a pretty good cook, and Mike seemed to enjoy the variety her style of cooking had brought to their diet. Liv had found Mike's cooking passable but a little too predictable. Still, she didn't take over the kitchen. They could blend their styles and share each other's tastes. There was something about working together that was strengthening a bond between them. Steve never stepped foot in the kitchen. He considered cooking to be 'woman's work' despite the fact that she was also the breadwinner in the family. Funny, at the time his behavior hadn't bothered her, but now she wondered why it hadn't.

After dinner, Mike said "Okay, we had a set-back today, but that was my fault. I was going about this the wrong way. I should have realized the city folk aren't cut out to be entrepreneurs, but the farmers already are. They were in business for themselves, making decisions without having to wait for some corporate big-wig upstairs to tell them what to do next. They've had to decide what materials to buy, how to market their products and balance their budgets. They already understand the basics of business. I just have to convince them to diversify. And their wives aren't idly sitting around. I wouldn't be surprised if they're not also involved in some of those business decisions. Family farms are family businesses."

"That's true, but... They might have been independent businessmen before the blackout but I got the impression they take their marching orders from their Bishop now. You'd have to get Joshua's 'blessing' before any of them would cooperate. You said you thought he wanted his town to return to its agrarian roots. Do you think you can sell him on your ideas?"

Mike was silent for a moment before he uttered a quiet "No."

After another long silence, he said "Maybe I can't, but I think I know of someone who could. Joshua and Sandra seem to go way back, and I got the distinct impression she has a crush on him. I can't get a read on him to know if he feels the same way, but I do know he is protective of her. If we could persuade Sandra, she might be able to influence him."

"Hey, 'ke-mo sah-bee', I noticed you said 'we' could persuade Sandra. Not that I want to play Tonto to your Lone Ranger, but how about telling me what you think my role in this will be."

"I don't think of you as Tonto - you're much better looking. Now that you mention it, though, I kinda like that you think of me as the Lone Ranger." Liv was shaking her head from side to side – but smiling.

"Okay, maybe not, but like I said, Joshua is protective of Sandra. I can't approach her, but you could."

"Hmm...she *was* friendly at the meeting Saturday. I suppose I could drop in on her tomorrow. I won't make you any promises. I hardly know her, so I can't just tell her what we're thinking unless I get the impression she might be receptive to it. Let me get to know her better first. Damn! Now I wish we *had* picked up my car. Oh, well. I guess I'll be chauffeuring you to work in the limo again tomorrow."

"It's not a limo."

"No, it's much bigger than a limo."

They laughed together. It felt as if they had always been together.

Chapter 14 – The Others

The next morning, Liv was up before Mike. She was ready to handle her assignment, but Mike didn't have one. Not only was his plan for a new economy failing, but he was beginning to wonder if the water project would fail, too. Joshua had sent children out to do the work of adults, and aside from Jonathon, the men at the plant were about as useful as children.

Liv sensed the change in Mike's mood. "Did you get up on the wrong side of the bed? Or worse, did you sleep *on* the bed or *under* it?"

"I guess I'm a little disappointed in the way things have been going – or not going, lately."

"You don't impress me as a quitter, so don't disappoint *me*! I'm counting on you. I'm going to talk to Sandra, like you asked. Meanwhile, you are going to go to the plant and make sure that project succeeds!"

Mike looked under the table where she was sitting, then looked down at his own legs.

Liv looked at him as if he had lost his mind. "What are you doing?"

Grinning, he replied "I was checking to see which of us was wearing pants today."

When Liv dropped Mike off at the plant he was in a better mood than he had been earlier. She had that effect on him a lot lately, and he was glad she was in his corner.

Jonathon hadn't arrived yet, and the other men were just sitting around waiting to be told what to do. Mike's good mood was fading fast. He thought how silly he had been to think they would ever show enough initiative to run their own businesses. They couldn't even muster enough initiative to work for others! Well, he was not going to tolerate this. Mike barked out orders to each of them and, although they didn't look pleased, they did at least start to perform the duties he had given them.

Mike wasn't any happier than they were. This was not his management style. Before the blackout, he had managed a hand-picked team of men and women who knew how to do what they were paid to do. He didn't have to micro-manage them. All that was necessary was to give them an overview of what needed to be done, and he could trust them to find the best ways to accomplish the tasks. Mike would not want to work for someone who didn't trust him to work independently, so Mike treated his team the way he would want to be treated. If he were picking a team for this current project, he wouldn't have hired any of these people!

When Jonathon arrived a few minutes later, he seemed surprised to find so many people actually working. "It looks like you lit a fire under them!"

"I was tempted to set fire to the whole lot of them! Now that they're doing something useful for a change, maybe you and I can discuss the problem we've been ignoring. We need a more permanent power source. These generators run on propane, and we don't have a lot of it. We'll be able to get the pumps up and running long enough to test the system and check for leaks, but what's the point if we can't provide a steady supply of water to everyone?"

"The youth have been scouring the town for more fuel while turning off water valves. We know where we can get quite a bit more now, but it will only keep things going for four or five weeks. It's a start, but you're right. We need a renewable power supply. What do you think about solar?"

"I built my own solar array. I know how to build solar panels and how to wire them, but I *bought* the solar cells. I can't make *them*. We also need a lot of batteries and a few power inverters. I don't suppose the youth have discovered a cache of those, have they?"

Their conversation was interrupted when Joshua burst into the office followed by two very agitated teenagers, a boy and a girl. "I knew this was too dangerous! I was opposed to this whole idea from the beginning. These two youths were attacked by men with guns! I should have never allowed you to talk us into endangering our youth!"

Mike wasn't going to let this rant go unchallenged. "I warned all of you of the potential dangers. You might recall that I suggested each team carry a weapon. I expected those teams to be made up of adults. You endangered the children, Joshua."

"They are not children, they are teenagers and they wanted to help. Besides, the adults have work to do. They couldn't be spared."

Mike decided arguing with Joshua was a waste of energy. He turned to the two kids and asked "Are you okay? Was anyone injured?"

The boy answered "No, they fired in the air to scare us. It worked! We jumped on our bikes and rode as fast as we could, all the way back to the church."

"Good. Good that you weren't hurt and good that it seems they didn't *want* to hurt you. Now, tell me exactly where this occurred, so I can go try to talk with those men. But before I go, I would like to ask you a few more questions. Anything you can tell me might make negotiating with them a little easier, okay?"

Both teens nodded in agreement.

"Okay. Let's see what else we know about them besides the fact that they have guns. Have you ever seen them before?"

"No, but we've never been out that far."

"Did it look like they lived there, or were they travelling? Did you see any cars or trucks?"

"They were in the farm house. There were trucks around."

Mike turned to Joshua. "Do you know anything about these people?"

"Yes, we've encountered them before. They have not been friendly to our missionaries. They rarely come into town for supplies. I believe they are ex-military."

Mike was fuming. He tried to keep his temper in check, but he couldn't keep from saying "You knew all that, and yet you sent these two kids out there alone!?! And you had the nerve to accuse *me* of 'endangering our youth'!"

"I suggest you watch your tone. Mike. I accepted you into our community. I've fed you and given you the opportunity to become a useful member of our society. This is how you repay my kindness?"

Mike was not usually a violent person, but he was close to punching this pompous ass in the face. Getting a grip on his rapidly rising temper, Mike managed to regain enough composure to say "You and I are overdue for a long conversation, but this is neither the time nor the place. If we are going to get water to 'your' community, I need to reason with those men now. So you can stay here and preach to someone who is willing to listen. I have work to do."

As he made what he hoped was a 'grand exit', Mike realized he didn't have a car! So much for his grand exit. He turned to Jonathon, since he couldn't say anything more to Joshua, and asked if there was a vehicle he could borrow.

Jonathon looked pleased at the opportunity to get away from the situation. He practically jumped out of his chair and led the way to where a utility truck was parked. As Mike drove away, he noticed Jonathon was still standing there. He didn't look like he was in any hurry to rejoin the Bishop.

The truck had almost half a tank of gas, assuming the gauge could be believed. That would be plenty for the round trip – if he was able to return. Mike had his Glock with him, but a shoot-out with several armed men was not what he had in mind. He was glad Liv had his car. This truck looked official, and it might give some credence to what he had to tell those men. Then again, if these guys were preppers they might also be anti-establishment. Suddenly, Mike realized being 'official' just might get him killed.

He debated the pros and cons as he drove up the dirt road that led to the farm. He decided 'official' was the way to play this, so he drove – slowly – up to the farmhouse, stopped a reasonable distance from it and tapped the horn. He kept the motor running, pulled up the parking brake and slipped the gear shift into reverse in case he had to move quickly.

Two men came out of the house and walked toward him. They were both carrying AK-47's, which made his Glock about as useful as a water pistol. Since using the gun would be futile, he figured he would seem less threatening if he was unarmed so he unclipped the holster from his belt and slid the holster and gun under the seat before they reached him.

"Hello, I'm from the water company. We're trying to get the water flowing again, but we have to make sure everyone's faucets are shut off first, so we sent some kids out here to check. You sure scared the hell out of them."

One of the men spoke. "You're from the government?"

"No, there's no government anymore - at least not that I can tell. It's just a bunch of town folks got together to try to fix a few things, that's all."

"Are you one of them Mormons?"

"Nope, but just because a bear shits in the woods doesn't mean I want to, and I can't make the toilet flush all by myself, so I got the Mormons to help."

That last line had just the effect Mike was hoping for. Both men were laughing, and they slung their weapons over their shoulders. "Okay, but why do we have to shut our faucets? No water will come out that way!"

The other man explained "If a bunch of faucets are open, too much water will flow too fast and they'll lose pressure. It'd also be a waste of water."

Mike said "Hey, I could use you down at the plant! You wouldn't believe the schmucks I have to work with!"

The first man spoke again. He was clearly their leader. "We haven't exactly had good relations with your Mormon friends, so we won't be helping out at your plant, but we can help at this end. I guess those kids won't be coming around this way again, so we could finish up where they left off."

"That would be a big help, thanks. The easiest way to do it is to shut off the main valves at each water meter. There are a lot of empty houses, and nobody wants to go inside them. The kids were just looking for your meter when you scared them off. I can loan you one of these special wrenches that fit the mains if you're willing to finish what they started. I've got their map here, so you can see what's left to do. My name's Mike, who am I talking with?"

"I'm Jake. We'll finish this. I'd like to have a flush toilet, too."

The other man said "Yeah and maybe we could convince you to take a shower! You stink, Jake!"

"Hey, the reason you can smell it is because it's closer than you think. I didn't want to say anything, but that odor is coming from *your* body."

"Ha-ha. Seems you guys know each other pretty well. I'm guessing you were in the service together, right?"

"Yeah, Special Forces in Iraq and Afghanistan. If you don't mind my saying, you look a little too old for combat, Mike."

Mike chuckled. "Uh-huh, but I wasn't too old for Nam. You look a little young. Maybe you never heard of Nam."

"Touché. Were you an officer?"

"Staff Sergeant, USAF. I saw combat, but unlike you guys I had a bird's eye view."

"Well, as long as you're not an officer, I guess you're OK. We'll get this done. I'll bring the wrench back to you tomorrow so you'll know when we're finished."

"Sounds good. Thanks. See you tomorrow."

Once he was back on the main road, Mike thought to himself "That went pretty well. See Mike, you had nothing to worry about." Still, a flush toilet would have come in handy right about then - and a change of clothes, too.

Chapter 15 – Plan B

Mike was pleased to find Joshua was gone by the time he arrived back at the plant. Jonathon cornered him as soon as he arrived. "You had me worried!"

"Thanks, but those guys out there aren't as scary as we were led to believe. Once I explained what we're trying to do, they were on board right away. They're going to finish what the kids didn't get to."

"Oh, uh, I didn't mean them. I was talking about when you confronted Joshua. I was afraid he was going to pull the plug on our operation! I mean, I'm glad you made it back safely, of course."

"Jonathon, I don't get it. You are a very capable engineer. You don't need Joshua's permission to do something that's going to benefit all of us! Why is everyone so afraid of Joshua?"

"He's our Bishop! You're not LDS, so maybe you don't understand. He is our leader. We have to do what he tells us to do – and *not* do what he tells us *not to do*."

"I get that. I'm a firm believer in governance by consent of the governed. His authority comes from all of you because, by joining the Church, you have consented to be governed by him. But I haven't given him my consent. He has no authority over me. However - and this is important - whenever those in authority fail to meet the needs of the governed, the people have a responsibility to speak up. You know this project is the right thing to do. Are you seriously saying that you would stop if he told you to stop?"

"I wouldn't just give up that easily. No, I would try to reason with him. But if I couldn't convince him, I would have to respect his decision. I would risk ex-communication if I did otherwise! Since the blackout, there's even more at stake now. Mike, I'm not a farmer. Without Joshua's support, my family would go hungry. Please consider all the ramifications here before you jeopardize the well-being of the rest of us."

"Point taken. I promise to keep that in mind, Jonathon." Mike had been entertaining a dream of a new free-market economy. There's nothing like a splash of cold, hard facts to dissolve a man's dreams! He realized that none of these people – city folks or farmers – were going to follow him unless Joshua did. It may all depend on Liv, now. Mike couldn't wait to hear how her visit with Sandra had gone.

The day dragged on until 4PM finally arrived. Mike was outside before Liv pulled up. She got out, walked around to the passenger's side and said "You drive! And please, let's go get my car!"

"Yes, Ma'am! I'll drive while you tell me about Sandra."

"You're not going to like it, but here it is. Sandra is an only child. That's rare for Mormon families, I know, but her parents died in a car crash when she was two. Her Aunt and Uncle took her to their farm, but then her Aunt died of cancer when Sandra was six. This poor kid never knew her mother and barely knew her surrogate mother! It's no wonder she's socially inept". Liv paused, thinking about the life Sandra had led.

"Oh, and you were completely wrong about her having a crush

on Joshua. He's her cousin! He was more like a big brother to her while she was growing up, and I guess he still is. She idolizes him, and I doubt if she would ever question his decisions or his actions. Also, she doesn't have a political bone in her body, and no detectible understanding of economics, either. She was studying nursing before the blackout. She cares about people, and would probably make a good nurse, but she will defer to Joshua's opinion on business issues."

"In other words, we're not going to get any help from her."

"Well, no we won't, but don't get me wrong. I like her. She is a sweet, innocent young lady." Then, in noticeably softer voice, she added." I'd like to think, if I had a daughter she would be like Sandra."

To Mike, the news was doubly bad. Not only had his last hope been dashed, but now it seemed some sort of previously dormant motherly instinct had been awakened in Liv as a result of her encounter. If Liv and Sandra expanded on this newly created relationship, and if Sandra was firmly planted in Joshua's camp, could Mike end up losing Liv's support?

Liv interrupted Mike's unpleasant reverie. "While Sandra and I were talking, some teens came in talking about a shoot-out. Do you know anything about that?"

"Yeah, it's a long story, but fortunately one with a happy ending. We're at your old house, so I'll tell you all about it when we get home. Let's see if we can get your toy car started."

The BMW responded nicely to a jump start, and the gas gauge showed three-quarters of a tank. That was more gas than the Caddy had left, so getting her car was a good idea. She followed him home and pulled into the other garage stall after Mike opened the door for her. "I'm sure I've got a clicker for your door somewhere. I'd better look for it now, or you'll be stuck in the garage."

After they both gave Plato the attention he deserved, Liv started dinner while Mike rummaged through his desk drawers. They ate early because cooking had to be done at least a few hours before sunset to give the solar array enough time to recharge the batteries for the night.

"I found it!" Mike said with more enthusiasm than seemed warranted, but after the crushing day he'd had, he was ready to get excited over the smallest of victories.

Over dinner, he told Liv about his adventures. If he exaggerated his confrontation with Joshua, it could be considered justifiable compensation for his lack of candor when he described his encounter with Jake. Mike had been scared, and a man doesn't tell his woman he was scared.

Liv listened quietly until Mike had finished his tale. "So, if this Jake character and his band of not-so-merry men are helping us, what else do you think they might be willing to do for us?"

"I like the way you think. That's not the only thing about you that I like, but it's pretty high on the list. It's a long list, by the way, but you probably don't want to hear it."

"Oh, that's okay, I have plenty of time. Tell me, tell me!"

"As a lawyer, you know anything I say can be used against me, so I think I'll take the Fifth. I will tell you this much, though. I like your laugh. And I like that you make *me* laugh. The rest will just have to remain a secret for now".

"Well, if you're going to be that way, I'm not going to tell you all the things I like about you. I've got a list too, you know."

"That's nice to hear. We'll have to compare notes someday." Mike would've liked nothing better than to forget all their problems and just talk about those lists, but he had to find a way to make life better for both of them, first.

"Anyway, I was thinking along the same lines you were. While I was out at Jake's place I noticed a few things. They have a solar array. It looks home-made, pretty much like mine, so one of those guys knows how to build them. I also noticed a tanker truck. You know - the type they used to use to deliver fuel to gas stations. They probably 'commandeered' it, but it means they have gas. That's something we're running low on. I also saw a radio tower. I think it might be a CB antenna, and I really wanted to ask if they could communicate with the outside world but I thought I'd better not ask a lot of questions yet. Jake promised to bring the wrench back tomorrow, so until I know his word is reliable, I didn't say much. I'm going to have a chat with him tomorrow. If he shows up, that is."

Chapter 16 – Plan C

Mike was up early Wednesday morning. If Jake and his buddies proved to be reliable, all sorts of possibilities might open up. The Mormons and the Special Forces boys wanted nothing to do with each other, which meant Mike could negotiate with Jake without worrying about Joshua knowing anything. Things were looking up again...maybe. He was getting ahead of himself. He knew next to nothing about Jake. "Don't get your hopes up, Mike. You have a lot of investigating to do first." Plato looked up, wondering if Mike was talking to him. Since Liv moved in, Mike hadn't been talking to himself as much as he had been, and Plato was confused.

As he was heading for the door, Liv came down the stairs.

"Hey, didn't you get the memo? Your chauffeuring gig has been cancelled. You are once again a lady of leisure, so you could have slept in."

"Can't a lady get up and see her man off to work? Okay, I confess I didn't get up *entirely* for your sake. I invited Sandra over for a visit today. She's such a sweet girl. But I also thought you're day might be a little brighter if I kissed you good-bye before you went off to work." And then she kissed him! Not a peck on the cheek, but an actual kiss! He put his arms around her, not wanting this to end. She caressed his face and they continued to kiss.

Mike would have been willing to quit his 'job' and spend the day at home, but Liv eased out of his embrace after a few wonderful moments. "Mmm, that's nice, but you have to go. Sandra will be here soon. She won't stay much past lunch, so if you can come home early today, we can...or... whenever you get home, I'll be here."

He couldn't stop smiling. In fact he had to consciously wipe the silly grin from his face as he entered the plant.

Mike wasn't late, but some people had arrived early. He found Jonathon and asked "What's going on. I haven't seen this place this busy since I barked at everyone the other day. What did you do?"

"Before we were interrupted yesterday, I was telling you the teens had located some fuel. We've been bringing it in. Mike, I think we're finally ready to test the system. Have you heard from you new friend, Jake? We can't start until we know everything is shut off out his way."

"He said he'd bring the wrench back when he's finished. Maybe he dropped it off. Did you see a wrench by the door?"

"No. I guess we'll have to wait."

"Let's give him another hour. If he isn't here by then, I'll drive out there."

They only had to wait twenty minutes. "Hey, is Mike here?" It was Jake, looking like he'd been mud-wrestling.

"Over here, Jake. What happened to you? You didn't look this bad the last time I saw you!"

"Aah, the last meter we tried to shut – it's always the last one that gives you trouble – the valve was rusted and the damn pipe broke. We had to dig a trench and rip out about ten feet of pipe. Then we had to find something to replace it with, find a welding torch… But I said we get it done, and it's done. Here's your wrench."

Jonathon stepped forward. "Jake, I'm Jonathon. I want to thank you. If our kids had run into a problem like that, we'd be screwed. Thank God you knew how to fix it!"

"You're welcome, but I'll never understand you people. You thank God when a person fixes something, but it never occurs to you to wonder why an all-powerful God didn't just prevent the damn pipe from breaking in the first place."

Mike cut Jake off with "Well, never mind. All's well that ends well, right?" and then ushered Jake out before anyone had a chance to respond.

"Jake, I want to thank you for all your efforts. You are a man of your word, and I respect that. Would it be alright if I drove out to your place later? We'll be turning the water on for a test run soon, and people will be running all over town checking to see if everything is working. I'll assign myself to your area. While I'm there, I'd like to talk to you about some other things we might be able to do to make life a little more normal around here, but I don't want to discuss it in front of these people."

"That's fine with me. I don't have much to say to these people anyway. I didn't do this for them."

As Jake drove away, Mike went back in. Everyone was celebrating. Mike thought that was premature. They didn't know yet if any of their efforts were actually going to work, but spirits were higher than they had ever been. He decided *that* was reason enough to celebrate.

By noon, they were ready to test their makeshift pumping system. The generators were running and the valves were open. There was a lot of air in the pipes, but after a few minutes there was clean water flowing. It was time to spread out around town and take pressure readings. The men ran to their bicycles. Mike took the utility truck he had driven yesterday. This was 'official business', and he wasn't going to waste the little bit of gas left in the Caddy. Before going to Jake's, he drove home.

L iv and Sandra were frightened when they heard his key in the front door lock. Plato stopped barking when he realized it was Mike, but he looked a little embarrassed for not knowing. Liv said "Oh, it's you! I didn't expect you home this early. Why didn't you come in through the garage?"

"Long story, but we got the water turned on and…"

Sandra jumped up. "Is the water really on? I should go home."

"For now, but I don't know for how long. We're running tests."

As Liv and Sandra said their hasty good-byes, Mike went out to the garage and turned on the water heater. By the time he got back, Sandra was gone. "Liv, I turned on the water heater. Please drain that dirty water out of the tub. Wait about an hour and then fill it with hot water. It won't actually be hot, but it ought to be warm – and clean! After you've filled the tub, I wouldn't blame you if you took a relaxing bath. I'll be gone for a few hours."

"Oh, I could kiss you…again!"

"Better not. If you do, I won't want to leave, and I really have to go. Can I get a rain-check?"

"Sure, but only if you promise to redeem it when you get back."

"Oh, I will, I will!"

On the drive out to Jake's, Mike passed a few men testing the mains as they had been instructed to do. That camaraderie at the celebration earlier had been a good sign. People were taking their responsibilities seriously for a change.

Mike honked the horn as he approached Jake's house. He was still a little leery of Jake's friends, and he didn't want anyone shooting at him. Jake came out to meet him. "Did it work?"

"It seems like it. Honestly, I don't know if we built up enough pressure to reach you way out here, but turn on just one faucet and let's see what comes out."

The pressure was weak, but the flow was steady. Jake yelled to the others, and they all started filling bottles. These guys weren't stupid. A bath would be nice, but fresh drinking water was more important.

As an apology, Mike said. "It's not great, but it's a start. Just so you know, this is just a test. We'll be shutting it off at four o'clock, or sooner if anything goes wrong. If we don't find any leaks, we'll turn it on again tomorrow. Have you still got that zone map I gave you yesterday?"

"Yeah, we don't throw anything away. Why?"

"There are five major zones on the map. We're asking everyone to take turns tomorrow. Zone One will draw water from 6AM to 8AM. Zone Two from 8 to 10, and so on. If everybody follows that schedule, you should have a lot more pressure when it's your turn."

"That makes a lot of sense. It can work, if people obey the rules. Americans are spoiled, though. They expect everything to work at the flip of a switch. In most parts of the world, rationing is commonplace. We've been in lots of places where water was rationed the way you're doing it. They rationed electricity the same way. But it looks like nobody gets water after 4PM?"

"Somebody has to man the generators and the pumps. Everybody goes home at four. Besides, we're using gas-powered generators and we don't have a lot of fuel. I think we need to replace them with some kind of renewable source. I built my own solar array at my house and I see you did, too. The trouble is, I can build panels but I'd need solar cells to build more. That's what I wanted to talk with you about."

"Mike, we aren't here to give stuff away. We'll pay for the water, but we don't want to partner up with the Mormons. We try to be self-sufficient, but when we can't, we don't ask for charity. We helped you because you were helping us, but mostly we just want to be left alone."

"I feel the same way. The bishop has been supplying us with food in exchange for my help. I consider it wages, but I don't want to be dependent on him and his Socialist scheme any longer than I have to. I'm a free-market Capitalist at heart, and I'm thinking of ways to build some businesses so we can buy and sell what everyone needs. The key to it all is getting some power sources. Solar is just the starting point. Will you hear me out?"

"You had me at 'free-market Capitalist'. Keep talking."

"Okay, the way it stands, about half of the people are farmers or ranchers. They are productive and the other half aren't. The Bishop has coerced the farmers to give up half their crops to feed the other half of the people. As you can imagine, the farmers are none too happy with this, but they're obeying their Bishop – so far. The farmers have tractors and other equipment sitting idle because they've run out of fuel. If they could get fuel, they could more than double their output. If they could produce twice as much, they would only have to give up a quarter of their crops to satisfy the Bishop, and they'd have a lot of food left over for trade – to buy fuel and maybe some other things we could offer for sale".

Jake had been listening, but as Mike paused, Jake said "I understand, but that's their problem. What's it got to do with us?"

"You might think that has nothing to do with you, but here's where you come in. There's a lot of gas and diesel sitting in underground storage tanks beneath gas stations. It's just sitting there, because the gas pumps don't work. If you could take over a station and set up a solar array, you could sell fuel to the farmers for their equipment. They could pay for the gas by selling their crops. Are you with me so far?"

A few of the other men had gathered around. One of them spoke up. "Hi Mike, my name is Martin and I'm no economist but I can balance a checkbook – which is more than a lot of people can do. I've got a couple of questions, if you don't mind."

"Shoot."

"The first problem I see is... this is sort of a 'which came first, the chicken or the egg' situation. How are the farmers gonna pay for the gas before they grow the crops? The second problem is... what are we using for money?"

"Martin, you've got a better grasp of the situation than most of the economists I've read. My answer to the second question should answer the first one. US dollars are useless. They're backed by the full faith and credit of a government that, as far as I can see, doesn't exist anymore. A lot of people bought gold and silver for a situation like this, but you can't eat gold, so why would anybody trade food for gold? It's funny, but I used to be one of those guys who thought we should go back on the gold standard, but not anymore. What I'm going to say may sound crazy, but hear me out and think about it for a minute."

"We're listening."

"Okay, when you used a credit card, your account was charged, or debited, and the seller's account was credited with a sum of money, but no actual money changed hands, right?"

"Right. It was just electronic transfers of numbers we called dollars, but no one used paper money much." Obviously, Martin was their spokesman for monetary matters. Everyone else just nodded when he spoke.

"So, we can keep track of debits and credits without having to have any kind of currency. Now, when someone wanted to start a business, they usually had to borrow some funds to get started. In our scenario, that means the farmers start out in debt because they have to buy fuel, so they need a 'loan' to do that. When they sell their crops, they'll get credits, which will allow them to pay back the loan. Meanwhile, whoever is running the gas station gets credits when he pumps the fuel. He can use those credits to buy food when the crops come in or for something else right away. It's his money, so he can use it any way he wants. But I need to take one step back. The person who builds the solar array for the gas station earns credits first. The person who owns the gas station starts out in debt because he can't earn any credits until the pumps work. Does that make sense?"

"It does, but who's going to be the banker?"

"Heh-heh, well who's idea was it? I'm pretty good with numbers. I've run a few successful businesses and helped other people run theirs. Also, my *uh* girlfriend was a lawyer. That's funny, too, because it used to be I didn't have much use for lawyers until I met Liv. But she can help by writing contracts for us so we all know where we stand. We'll be a virtual bank. If everyone can agree, I would charge a fee on each sale the way Visa charged for every transaction we all conducted with our credit cards, but I won't charge any interest on the loans. It's like Martin said about the chicken and the egg. This won't work without loans, so nobody should have to pay a price to get one. The only condition would be that you can't get a loan unless you are going to offer something for sale. You may have figured out, too, that no one can buy anything unless they've either gotten a loan or they work for someone who pays them in credits. A free market works when everybody involved has to rely on everybody else to keep it going. *Now*, what do you think?"

Jake was the first to answer. "I'm not too comfortable having to deal with the Mormons."

"I understand, but you don't have to like somebody in order to trade with them."

Martin was still thinking. Finally, he asked "Who sets the prices?"

"Nobody gets to 'set' prices. You may have heard this before, but I think it's worth repeating. The right price is what the buyer is willing to pay and the seller is willing to accept. No sale happens until the buyer and seller agree on a price, no matter what's being bought and sold."

"Okay, just so I understand it, walk me through how a sale happens."

"Each member of our economic community will have a debit card. After the buyer and seller reach an agreement, the buyer hands the seller his debit card and the seller charges the agreed-upon amount. And just like Visa, we charge the buyer's account and credit the seller's account for the amount they settled on – minus our 4% fee. We keep a record of every sale, so ownership of the goods is established, and we give everybody a monthly statement so you know how much you've got that you can spend and how much you still owe on your loan, if you had one. If there's ever a dispute over a sale, Liv will provide arbitration to settle the matter. There's no need for courts or governments, which also means there's no sales tax or income tax."

Everyone was nodding in agreement now. Mike wanted to get some sort of commitment from them before he left here today, so he continued. "Like I said before, nothing can happen without some kind of power source. There is a solar panel manufacturer in South Phoenix. They must have solar cells in stock, and maybe some panels already built. I'm thinking someone ought to conduct a commando raid on that plant." And with a big grin, he said "Do you know anybody who could pull that off?"

That caused a lot of laughter. Finally, Jake – still laughing - said "But Mike, wouldn't that be illegal?"

"Tell you what...next time I see a cop, I'll be sure and ask him. Meanwhile, do you think you could find some solar cells that nobody is using?"

"I know the place you're talking about. The freeways are clogged, and the surface streets aren't much better, but we'll give it a try. Check back with us next Monday."

"Hey, speaking of checking in... I don't want to get too far ahead of myself, but...You guys were a commando unit, so I'm guessing one of you is a communications expert."

"That would be Radar. We've called him that for so long, I can't remember his real name. Radar, front and center! The Sarge has got some questions for you."

"Just one... If we could power up a cell tower, could you establish local phone service? I don't mean streaming videos. Just your basic talk and text will do."

Radar thought a moment and said "We'd need two towers, minimum. Four would be better. Then, we have to reprogram all the phones to be compatible. It can be done, yes."

"Okay, there's another business. People would pay for the ability to stay in touch with each other without having to pedal their damn bicycles everywhere. Congratulations, Radar, you are about to become an entrepreneur! Which one of you is the best auto mechanic?"

Mike realized he should have phrased that question differently, because every one of them was claiming to be better than everyone else. Finally, the matter was settled and Sam was nominated.

"Sam, you should be the one who owns the gas station. Once people can buy gas, they'll need someone to keep their vehicles serviced. This is gonna work, guys, but only if you want it to. What do ya say?"

Jake answered for everyone. He was definitely their leader.

"Like I said, check back with us on Monday. We'll let you know then."

"Fair enough, I'll see you Monday."

Mike had to check in with Jonathon. He would have preferred to just go home to Liv, but he had to switch vehicles anyway, so he drove back to the plant. The two men agreed the test had been successful, and the water would be on at 8AM tomorrow. It was finally time to go home.

He couldn't wait to tell Liv how well things were shaping up, but before he had the chance, she said "I really enjoyed bathing in clean water again. Why don't you take a shower? I'm sorry you're getting the water second-hand, but it's a lot cleaner than it was this morning!"

"Yeah, a shower sounds good."

"Great. And when you're finished, don't bother to get dressed."

He could always tell her tomorrow.

Chapter 17 – A Clash of Ideologies

Thursday morning was different. For one thing, Mike thought the bed felt more comfortable. It was a nice mattress, and he'd never had any reason to complain about it, but sharing it with Liv changed his perception of a lot of things. It was definitely more comfortable now – softer and warmer, but a lot harder to get out of.

He had lived alone for such a long time that he had forgotten how passionate he could be with the right partner. Was it ever as good before as it had been last night? Mike wasn't sure. Memories are unreliable at best, but he thought this might be the best it had ever been. Not that the past mattered. This was a new beginning, and he just wanted to savor it.

Liv was physically attractive. Mike saw that the first time they met, even though she had been near death, lying in a parking lot. Since then, he had seen that she was a beautiful person inside, as well. Even if none of his plans worked out, he knew he would be happier with her than without her. He kissed her cheek.

But it was Thursday, another work day, and he had to get up.

The sound of the shower woke her. She had been having a most wonderful dream. In it, she and Mike had made love, and he was kissing her tenderly. She didn't want the dream to end. And then she thought to herself, this is a very comfortable bed. And she knew it hadn't been a dream.

She also thought Mike shouldn't have to shower alone.

******

Jonathon was annoyed that Mike arrived so late, but he knew he had no right to complain. Mike had been a tremendous help, and since he wasn't one of them, Jonathon could only accept the help Mike was willing to give. If he didn't want to continue, there was nothing Jonathon could do about it. Once he looked at it from that perspective, his annoyance disappeared and was replaced by relief. At least Mike hadn't quit!

"Good morning, Jonathon. How is everything going?"

"Fine, Mike, fine. We had everything running on schedule at eight. If everyone adheres to the schedule we gave them, there should be ample pressure to supply the whole town with clean water."

"Glad to hear it. Jonathon, now that you have everything under control, I think you should decide which of the men you want working for you permanently. You don't need all of us."

"You're forgetting... it's not up to me. The Bishop will decide who is to work here."

"Oh, c'mon Jonathon! The Bishop couldn't have done this without you. He's your spiritual leader, he's not an engineer. This is your operation. He will have to leave you in charge, or there won't be any water. He knows that. And if you are in charge, you should get to choose who works for you and who is no longer needed. Just tell him."

"Mike, he's feeding all these men and their families. I can't fire them!"

"If you let them go, do you really think he will stop feeding them? That's not going to happen. Let him worry about his welfare program. You need to concern yourself with what is best for your water company."

"It's not a company, it's…it's…I don't know what to call it, but it's not a private business."

"We'll see about that." Mike realized he was saying too much. He didn't know if Jake was on board yet, and until he could be sure, Jonathon was right. This was not a business…yet. "Anyway, what can I do to help this morning?"

Jonathon asked Mike to go over some figures with him, and they kept busy for the remainder of the morning until Joshua showed up with lunch. Seeing the food reminded Mike that he and Liv were still very much dependent upon the Bishop for now. He ate, even though he'd lost his appetite. He also took some food home, just as all the other men did.

As usual, Joshua consulted with Jonathon and Mike privately while they ate. Before Joshua left, Mike said "Turning the water on and off each day this way could cause problems that wouldn't occur if we could keep the pressure constant. I think I could be more useful in the field, spot-checking the main valves to be sure everything is tight. What do you think, Jonathon?"

"Someone should be doing that, and you are better qualified than anyone else. Thanks for offering."

"Fine, I'll come in every morning as usual and check in with you before making my rounds."

Joshua didn't look pleased that the decision had been made without consulting him. One way or another, Mike was going to get Jonathon accustomed to being in charge! Not to be left out of the conversation entirely, Joshua asked Mike "Will you not be here for lunch, then?"

"Maybe you could set some aside for me. I'll check in with Jonathon each afternoon before going home." And to make his point final, Mike started his new 'assignment' right away.

He was happy to be out of the plant. He'd check the valves as he said he would, but it wasn't really something that needed doing. He wanted to drive out to Jake's, but that would have to wait until Monday. It wouldn't be a good idea to rush those guys. He'd have to let them join him on their own terms, and for now those terms meant giving them the weekend to think about it.

Everything looked tight, just as he expected. At 3:45 he headed back to the plant. Jonathon was waiting for him, looking even more nervous than usual.

"Mike, the Bishop has decided the other men can check the valves starting tomorrow. He said your services are no longer needed – but he appreciates everything you did for us! He told me to tell you he'll be stopping by your house later with some food."

Of course! He should have seen this coming. Joshua *had* to employ his people in order to justify the food he gave them. Mike was expendable. Tonight, Joshua was going to give Mike his 'severance package'.

"Jonathon..." Mike wanted to berate the man for not standing up to Joshua, but what good would that do? Instead, he said "...It has been a pleasure working with you. Although I've been given my walking papers, don't hesitate to call me if you have a problem you think I might be able to solve. I'd be happy to help you. Your Bishop doesn't have to know about it. It'll just be two friends chatting, understand?"

"Yes, I understand, and thanks for the offer. I'm not sure I could keep it from the Bishop, but if I run into a problem I *will* call on you!" They shook hands and parted as friends.

Mike headed home to tell Liv to expect a house guest - and that he had been fired.

Liv greeted him as he walked in from the garage. She looked terrific, and Mike hated to have to spoil whatever plans she had for this evening. He couldn't resist kissing her, but pulled away quickly. "Liv, I have a lot to tell you, and not much time to tell it in, so sit down, please."

"What's happened?"

"Now that the water is flowing, there's no need for all of us to show up every day. Joshua has to keep his church members busy so he can convince the farmers to keep feeding them, so he sort of fired me."

"That ungrateful son-of-a..." Mike stopped her. "Honey, if I were in his shoes, I would have done the same thing. Of course, I would never allow myself to *be* in his shoes, but that's another matter. He's coming over sometime this afternoon, bringing us some food. I think it's his way of softening the blow. Since he doesn't like to be out after dark, he's probably on his way now. I never had a chance to tell you about my meeting with Jake yesterday, but that will have to wait until Joshua leaves. Uh, you might want to change your clothes..."

"Oh! I'll just be a minute."

She had just reached the top of the stairs when there was a

knock on the door. Mike let Joshua in, helping him with the crate he had strapped to his horse.

"Thanks for the supplies, Joshua. If you have a few moments, I'd like to talk with you." Mike escorted the Bishop out to the patio, hoping that Liv would recognize that Mike wanted to talk privately.

"Joshua, you must know that all those men are not needed to run the water treatment plant. That many men weren't needed in the first place, but now Jonathon could handle things with one or two assistants."

"Yes, Mike, I know, but I don't think you understand the situation I'm in. I have to provide for them and I can't let them sit idle while we feed them."

"I think I DO understand your predicament. I'm not sure you do. How long do you think you can keep this up before the farmers rebel and refuse to feed the half of your ward that doesn't contribute anything useful to the community? They're grumbling already."

Joshua wanted to respond, but Mike interrupted. "But it's more than that. You are supposed to be their spiritual leader, but circumstances have put you in an awkward position. You have been seeing to the physical needs of people who are adrift without their previous means of support, but you're ignoring their emotional needs. You've given them food, but taken away their dignity!"

It took Joshua a few moments to respond. "Your evaluation of the situation is surprisingly accurate. Don't assume I'm not aware of the damage being done to their self esteem, but it is easier to identify a problem than it is to find a solution. My first responsibility was to ensure that they didn't starve! I sent them to the plant hoping they would feel useful, even though the work there would seem demeaning compared to their previous occupations. I did it as much for them as I did it to show the farmers that these people were not deadbeats. What more would you have me do?"

"Actually, I assumed that was the motivation for your actions. I'm not faulting you for what you've done so far, but you must know that it was only a stop-gap solution. Let's call what you did 'Phase One'. It was logical and appropriate, but sending them back to the plant now that most of the work has been accomplished tells me you don't have a plan for 'Phase Two'."

"I wouldn't go so far as to call it a plan, but I had hoped that a steady supply of water for irrigation would increase the crop yield. That would mean the farmers will get to keep more of what they produce while still seeing to the needs of the others. That should quell the 'grumblings', as you called it."

"It's a step in the right direction, but much more is needed. The men at the plant know they are not needed. Man lives by more than bread alone. How do you intend to fix that?"

"I honestly don't know. There have always been those among us less capable than others. It is our responsibility to see to their basic needs. I am doing that. I do not know how to provide them with a purpose in life. That should be for each individual to find for himself. But I suspect we wouldn't be having this conversation unless you thought you had an answer, so tell me what you would do."

"Everyone must find something they can produce that others

will want, so that they can trade for what they want but can't produce. This is the basis of free-market Capitalism."

"NO! Capitalism has destroyed the lives of so many people throughout history! I can't believe you would suggest such a thing. It is better that a man accept food given with love than to slave for wages that are insufficient to pay for the food his family needs."

"Heh-heh, I thought as much. You and I have different definitions of Capitalism. It's true, the sort of Capitalism you're thinking of – where a few wealthy Capitalists exploited the masses for profit - has been the bane of society many times in history. The outrageous behavior of a few bad apples has led to revolts by people who thought Socialism or Communism would be better. But those systems have also failed wherever they've been tried. Let me give you an example of the sort of system I had in mind." Joshua was listening, so Mike continued.

"Think of a wheat farmer. He grows his crops and sells his wheat to a baker. The farmer is a Capitalist. The baker bakes the wheat into bread and sells it to a mechanic. The Baker is a Capitalist. The mechanic has to buy bread because he is too busy repairing the farmer's tractors and the baker's delivery van to grow wheat or bake bread. Because he earns a living by using his mechanic skills, he is a Capitalist. Now, tell me. Which of these men is being exploited?"

"Well, none of them in your example, but not everyone possesses the skills to be what you call a Capitalist. For example, does the farmer have helpers who work to bring in the crops? Might they be exploited?"

"Yes and no. If someone never aspires to be anything more than an unskilled worker for his entire life, he will no doubt be exploited by someone eventually. But if that farm hand uses his time on that job to gain the knowledge and experience needed to start his own farm, he was not exploited – he was getting on-the-job training. The same would be true if someone went to work for the baker or the mechanic. He could someday be a baker or a mechanic himself, unless he lacked the drive to better himself. In a free-market economy, everyone is either a Capitalist or a Capitalist-in-training. There are no mega-corporations, just small business people and trainees. They used to be called 'Masters' and 'apprentices'."

"You're talking about the way things were hundreds of years ago. Don't you think we've progressed beyond those quaint ideas?"

"We have, but I'm not sure it was progress. Under that 'quaint' system, Masters only accepted apprentices that had both the innate aptitude and interest needed to succeed in that field. The apprentices learned because they really were interested and because they were not entirely inept. That system was replaced when everyone accepted the theory that all children should get an equal education – a Socialist concept, by the way. So we all learned Algebra and we all studied Shakespeare, even though some people have little aptitude for math or even less interest in ancient English literature. Once the students have completed twelve-plus years of drudgery, we declare them 'educated' and send them out to find jobs. Not meaningful, personally rewarding careers, but 'jobs' – usually jobs requiring no understanding of algebra or Shakespeare. Progress? I don't think so."

"So you would abandon formal education and have everyone learn on the job? There aren't enough jobs to go around and employers don't want to train people."

"That has been the case, and even getting a college degree didn't help. But that was true a few months ago. The world has changed drastically since then and we have an opportunity to build a new economy – one scaled down to fit the size of our current population. What will our children do if we don't teach them the skills needed in today's world? How will the next generation survive if they don't learn those skills?"

"This has been a very interesting philosophical discussion, but I don't see how it solves our immediate problems, Mike."

"It doesn't, but I'm trying to present a platform on which a solution can be built. You were thinking the same way I am when you thought increasing water flow would increase yield. I've seen tractors sitting idle at those farms, and I'm pretty sure yields would increase much more if we could provide fuel for the farmers' equipment. But unlike the water problem, getting fuel requires a few more steps. And I'm convinced Capitalism will solve this problem better than Socialism will. I don't have all the pieces together yet, but I have been working toward that goal. If you want, I'll give you an overview of what needs to happen to achieve it."

"I can't imagine how you are going to do what you say. We've gathered all the available fuel for use at the water plant. We've looked around. There is no more."

"You've looked around, but you haven't looked down. There's a lot of gasoline and diesel in underground storage tanks beneath every gas station, but we need electricity to pump it up. The only reliable source of electricity at our disposal is solar, but we need many more solar panels. I'm currently looking for a supply of those. I and some other people I know have the expertise to install them. If one of us builds a solar array at a gas station, that person will want to sell fuel. Farmers will want to buy that fuel. Since it will drastically increase their crop yield, they'll be able to afford the fuel and still continue to supply you with the amount of food you're receiving now. But, as a percentage of their total yield, you'll only be asking for an amount equal to what their tithe should normally be. No more grumbling!"

"So the farmers and the gas station attendant will be Capitalists. I suppose that's okay, but it doesn't solve all the problems we've agreed exist."

"No, there's much more. That's just a start. Once we've found a way to make most people self-employed and self-reliant, we could include Jonathon. He could 'own' the water business, employ some helpers and get paid by everyone who gets their water from him. That would be a few less to be fed by the Church. And, with a revenue source, he could buy fuel for the generators. Better still, he could buy solar, so we could save the liquid fuels for use in tractors, trucks and cars. The church can pay the water bill for those who haven't yet found the means to generate their own income."

"How can the Church pay? It doesn't sell anything."

"It doesn't have to. Once your church members become earners, you will of course ask them to tithe a percentage of their earnings to the Church. The more they earn, the more the Church can do for the less fortunate. Maybe in time, you could even pay the farmers for the food they give you."

"This is too simplistic. It sounds good, but your story lacks details. I don't see how you can make it work."

"There are a lot of details, and I'm sorry if my explanation was an oversimplification of the plan, but it's getting late and I know you won't want to stay much longer. For now, can we just agree to talk more another time?"

"We can, because I've enjoyed this conversation, but do not think you will convince me of the merits of Capitalism. I should warn you, I majored in Political Science. What you are saying conflicts with most of what I already know!"

"Ha-ha. And what they taught you conflicts with most of what I know. I look forward to our next discussion."

Liv had taken the hint and refrained from joining them. Now she said a polite hello and good-bye as the Bishop left.

"Well, neither of you look bloodied. Congratulations on keeping your composure. That couldn't have been easy! What did you two talk about?"

"I'd rather tell you about what Jake and I talked about. Hey, I'm starving! Did you eat?"

"No, I was waiting for you."

"Thanks. Let's eat. Then I'll tell you about our potential future."

Mike told Liv everything that went on at Jake's ranch, and what he had learned about the other men there. The more he talked, the more enthused he became.

Finally, she said "Whoa, ease up. I think I see the potential, but it sounds like nothing is a done deal yet. What if they just say no?"

"I'd rather not think about that possibility. Besides, I got a good vibe when I was there. They are a rough group of guys, but I think they are honest men. I think they'll be on board. But I won't know until Monday. Right now, I think we should go to bed. Uh, I'd like it if you'd join me, even if we don't try for a repeat performance of last night."

"We don't have to if you don't want to."

"Oh, I want to! I didn't want you to think I was taking anything for granted."

"Well, I guess I shouldn't, either. No matter what we end up doing though, I'd really like to sleep with you, even if we only sleep – if that's okay with you."

"I'm definitely okay with that. And, since I'm unemployed, we can sleep in tomorrow morning – and the next day, and the next day. In fact I wouldn't care if we didn't get out of bed until Monday!"

Well, that was an exaggeration. They would get out of bed, because there was a lot to do. With only a two-hour window of opportunity to get clean water, they needed to refill their store of drinking water, wash clothes, sheets, towels, dishes and clean the house. All of those things that we took for granted before, like clean clothes, were a luxury they had not enjoyed for a long time. But for Mike, the biggest improvement was that he could bring the toilet seat in from the yard and re-install it where it belonged!

Chapter 18– Rain, Rain, Go Away...

The weekend passed pleasantly enough. The chores didn't seem like work, doing them together. And the two of them worked well together, laughing most of the time.

It rained Sunday evening. Mike was glad he didn't have to catch rain water like the last time, but Liv was unusually quiet. It took Mike nearly an hour to understand why her mood had changed so drastically. The last time it rained, she had watched her husband fall to his death! He felt foolish for not realizing it sooner, and at the same time, helpless to 'fix' the problem. Somewhere from the depth of the trivial bits of information that cluttered his brain, he remembered reading that most men tend to want to solve problems, while most women preferred to be consoled. So, although it was out of character for him, he stopped talking and held her.

As soon as it started to rain, Liv was overcome with emotion. She tried not to think of that day, but the image of Steve's lifeless body lying in a puddle of blood and muddy water was impossible to erase. It didn't help that Mike kept talking about what he had to do when it rained before. He was rambling on about every detail of every step he would take to capture and filter the water. She thought *"Men can be so insensitive!"* Mike had seemed less obtuse than any man she had met before, but today...She tried to change the subject, but he just kept talking about the rain. This was the first time she was angry with him, but that anger might have been the only thing keeping her from crying.

Finally, he seemed to notice the pain she was in. The look on his face at that moment was one of compassion - not pity, but genuine love. Her anger melted away and she knew she was going to start crying. He took her in his arms just before the tears began to flow. This was just what she needed – the warmth of his caress, the release of her tears and the fact that he had finally stopped talking!

Chapter 19 – A Business Proposition

It had rained most of the night, and they had fallen asleep in each other's arms. By morning, the clouds had passed and so had the cloud hanging over Liv. She kissed him and said "Good morning. This is the big day! You have a meeting with Jake, right? Oh, and by the way, I love you."

"Wow! This really is a good morning!"

Mike insisted that Liv shower first. They had drained and refilled the tub yesterday, so the water was clean. They still used the recirculating shower system Mike had built because they weren't allowed to run water until 2PM. Things weren't back to normal yet, but they were getting better. Of course, Liv thought it was very chivalrous of him to let her have the first shower, and Mike let her believe that. She didn't need to know that he just liked watching her as she got out and toweled herself dry. Was he a dirty old man? Well, there was no denying he was old, and as for dirty...he told himself that wasn't his fault. He hadn't had a shower yet!

Mike had shed his paranoia a bit and re-installed the doggie door, so Plato didn't have to wait for Mike to let him out. Now Plato was outside, playing like a puppy in the puddles. Mike couldn't blame him. It rained so seldom here it must be a real treat for the dog. Considering Liv's reaction last night, Mike was grateful that it didn't rain more often. Mike closed the doggie door. Plato would just have to stay outside until he dried off.

Over breakfast, Mike and Liv discussed the sort of contracts that would be needed when (or if) people signed on to Mike's economic plan. Liv agreed to draft some documents while Mike was gone, and he headed to Jake's to see if any of it was worth the effort.

He stopped short of the ranch house and honked the horn, like he had done before, but was surprised at the reception he got today. Instead of a hearty welcome from Jake, he was confronted by several men pointing their weapons at him! What the hell? Oh, of course! They were used to seeing him in the utility truck. They didn't recognize the Caddy. He got out, waved and hollered "Hello, it's me, Mike. Is Jake here?"

"Hey, Mike, nice vehicle upgrade. Didja get a raise?"

"Hi, Sam, no, actually, just the opposite - I got fired. Now that we got the water working, my partnership with the Mormons has been terminated. No more perks, like a company truck. This old girl is mine. Ain't she a beauty?"

"Well it must be true, what they say. 'Beauty is in the eye of the beholder'. That beauty is a little past her 'sell by' date, ain't she?

"Hey, with less than 200,000 miles on her, she's barely broken in."

"Yeah, she looks to be in nice condition. I respect a man who takes care of his vehicles."

Sam would have been happy to talk cars all day, but Mike had other things on his mind. "Check her out if you want, but treat her gently. Is Jake inside? I'd like to talk to him."

"He's expecting you. Go on in." Sam said, as he popped the hood and lovingly admired the Northstar engine.

Jake was sitting at the table, poring over some hand-written paperwork.

"Hi, Jake, how did the mission go? Did you find any solar panels?"

"Oh yeah, I guess we did a good job of hiding the semi we've got out back. It's full of panels, cells and materials to build more panels. I was just crunching some numbers here. I hope you've got a plan to make all this worth our effort. You wouldn't believe what we went through to get that big rig here. The roads are mostly impassable, and we had to zig-zag half way around the county."

"Just out of curiosity, did you see any other survivors in your travels?"

"Lots of bodies, but none that were still breathing. It looks worse than Afghanistan. At least in a war, most people die quickly. These folks died slow, painful deaths from starvation and dehydration."

"Most people were completely unprepared. Not that anybody deserves to die that way, but they didn't do anything to avoid it."

"Yeah, from what we've been able to learn, very few were prepared. I expected there would be more. There may be, but we're only able to talk to the ones who have CB's, and there aren't many of them. I wish I had a Ham radio. Those babies have a much greater range than a CB."

"So that *is* a Citizen's Band antenna. I thought it might be. There used to be a lot of Ham radios when I was growing up, but with the Internet, most people lost interest in radio. I think they run on 12-volts, so if a guy's got a charged-up battery, he's got enough power to communicate. A friend of mine had one. I wish I did. Then I'd know if he was still alive. He only lives about 100 miles from here, but that might as well be on the other side of the planet."

"Maybe we can locate him for you. Do you know his handle?"

"Huh? Oh, you mean the name he uses. No, I don't."

"Then chances aren't good. Nobody uses their real name, and nobody is giving out any identifying info like their exact location. You never know who you're talking to or what their intentions might be."

"That's funny. It sounds a lot like on-line dating! Oh, well, let's get back to the solar situation. Did I explain how the economics would work?"

"Yeah, you're gonna give people loans to buy our installations if they use them to produce something they can offer for sale. So you'll give Sam a loan and we'll build an array at a gas station so he can sell fuel. We did some checking, and the Shell station's tanks are pretty low, but the Chevron station must have gotten a delivery just before the blackout, so Sam wants to use that one. It's an older station with two service bays that haven't been used for years, so he can set up shop there to do repairs."

"Good, I want all of you guys to enter into a contract as partners in the solar business, so payments will be made to your company and you can divide up the profits between you any way you want. Liv will draw up the contract for you, and also the sales agreements your buyers will have to sign. She'll leave the amount blank, because we won't know the price until you negotiate it with each customer. Since what you're selling will be a big-ticket item, you have to agree to accept installment payments. That makes it affordable for your customers and it also gives you a steady stream of income instead of boom and bust. Does that sound okay to you?"

"It sounds very professional, yeah, that's good. How are you going to get customers for Sam's business?

"The Bishop isn't too fond of my ideas. I'm going to talk directly with the farmers. They'll want to get their tractors running again. I think I also have a way to force the Bishop to cooperate, eventually. They don't have much fuel for the generators at the water plant, and he'll have a riot on his hands if the water stops flowing again."

"Well, you're a pretty convincing salesman, so if anybody can talk them into it, it's probably you. You're going to earn your 4%."

"I intend to! So, I'll bring Liv out here tomorrow to do the paperwork if you promise me she'll be safe. You guys have been alone out here for a long time." Mike tried to make that sound like a joke, but he was actually half-serious.

"Hey, we're not animals. Although I can't guarantee no one won't want to sniff her." Jake's good-natured grin was reassuring enough for Mike, but there was something else he had to ask.

"When Sam's station opens for business, I'm going to be one of his first customers. Meanwhile, can you make *me* a loan? I'm pretty low on gas and I think I saw a tanker out back. I hope it's got unleaded in it."

"It does. Drive around, the first tank's on us."

On the way back home, Mike decided to make his first sales call.

He'd passed a large farm on the way out that had several tractors that looked like they hadn't moved in awhile. Mike drove up, stopping short of the house and honking the horn as he did at Jake's. He wasn't at all surprised when people appeared, holding rifles.

"Hello, my name is Mike. You might remember me from the meeting we held on Saturday about the water."

"Yes, I recognize you. Wait there, I'll get my husband." She was cautious. He couldn't blame her. He'd wait. The wife had disappeared, but there were still two girls with their rifles aimed in his general direction. While he was waiting, he realized he had his Glock strapped to his waist, in plain sight, which was probably why they weren't putting their rifles down. It was too late to hide it. Oh, well, they might as well know he was as cautious and as prepared as they were.

The wife reappeared, saying "Show the man in, girls." They pointed the way and followed him in. Although Mike felt like he had just been taken prisoner, he didn't see that he much choice. He'd come this far, and he needed to see it through.

Harold looked to be in his late fifties or early sixties. It was hard to judge, because he was a man that had spent his life out in the harsh Arizona sun. Mike thought fifty-five was about right.

"We're grateful for your help getting us water. We have followed the schedule, not wanting to take more than is our rightful amount, but we could use more. Farming takes a lot of water. But we're expecting a bigger harvest with the water we've been given, so we're grateful."

"I was happy to help. We all appreciate running water. I want you to know I'm not involved with the plant now that the preliminary work is done. Jonathon is more than capable of handling it now, as long as he can get enough fuel to keep the generators running. I've been looking for ways to provide a better source of power for the plant, because none of us want the water to stop flowing."

"Amen to that! But what is it you think we can do for you? I imagine that's why you're here."

"No, actually I'm here because there may be something I can do to help *you*. I noticed some farm equipment that's not being used. I'm assuming you don't have any gas for them. If you could get fuel for your tractors, would that increase your productivity much?"

"Much? It would increase it five-fold! We can't plant most of our acreage by hand."

"With the amount of food the Bishop has been asking from you I imagine it's been hard getting by with what's left after feeding the rest of the Ward. So if you could buy gas, you could produce five times as much food. Would you be willing to sell that surplus to pay for gas – and for water, if we could offer more of it?"

"You're on the right track, Mike. The gas would let us use our equipment, but without more water we wouldn't be much better off than we are now. Are you saying you could supply us with both? How much will that cost me?"

Mike thought, *"I've gotten over the first hurdle. He's definitely interested, and he didn't say he'd have to ask the Bishop first, like Jonathon would have done. That's a relief. But now I have to explain the economics to him. Will he understand what I'm going to say?"*

Just then, a younger man stepped into the room. "I overheard what was said. I think he's suggesting that you could barter food for gas and water."

Harold replied "He hasn't said how it would work yet, Harry. Mike, this is my son, Harry. We named him Harold Junior, but he prefers Harry. He studied economics and he's handled our finances for the last few years, so why don't you continue this talk with him. I like the idea, but I've got fields to tend. If Harry says the price is right, you can count me in."

Harry didn't waste any time. "Barter is a very inefficient method of trade, Mike. I hope we can come to better terms than that."

Mike couldn't help smiling. "Harry, I couldn't agree more." As Mike explained his economic plan, Harry absorbed every detail with very few interruptions.

When Mike had run out of things to say, Harry said "That's quite a bit different from the monetary systems I learned in college, but I think it might be just the right thing for these different times we find ourselves in. What I like most about your plan is that by starting with nothing but a loan – at zero interest – no one has an economic advantage over anyone else. The rich can't squeeze out the poor because no one is rich or poor! If precious metals like gold or silver were used as currency, someone could corner the market and control all of us. You've designed a free-market Capitalist economy that would please a Socialist! It's the best compromise I've ever heard."

"Thank you. You know, it's ironic. I was one of the most vocal opponents of Bernanke's Quantitative Easing schemes because he was producing money out of thin air. And now, I discovered the only fair way to give everyone an even chance is to...create money out of thin air!"

"Ha, that is ironic, but while I also opposed the Fed's shenanigans, I support your plan. This is different. You're not giving the money to banks. If Bernanke had distributed the money he created the way you're proposing to do it, I would have supported him, too. How do we get started? I suppose you have some contracts to be signed."

"Not today, but I'll have the necessary paperwork drawn up tomorrow. Keep in mind, we are at the beginning stages of all this. The solar array hasn't been installed at the gas station yet, but work should start tomorrow. By the end of the week, Sam should be open for business. You will be able to buy gas or diesel then, but only after agreeing to sell some of your next harvest. You can't get a loan or become a buyer unless you commit to being a seller."

"I understand, although I'll have to read the contract first. As long as it matches what you've described, I see no problem."

"That's fine. Liv and I will come by tomorrow afternoon with the paperwork. I won't ask you to sign anything then. Take a few days to read it over, and then let me know if you have any questions or concerns. We've got until the end of the week before any sales can take place, so there's no hurry."

"One more question before you go. You said we would be able to buy water, too. That must mean you intend to sell fuel to the water treatment plant and ask it to sell water. If they start selling water, what happens to the people who aren't members of this deal? How do they buy water?"

"That, Harry, is one of the larger stumbling blocks I'm facing, and its name is Bishop Joshua. He and I have spoken, but we haven't found common ground yet. For now, let's go with the assumption that you will only be charged for more water than you're current allotment. That will need to change eventually, but...one step at a time."

They said their good-byes and Mike drove toward home, resisting the temptation to make another 'sales call'. Harold had one of the largest farms in the area and was probably influential in the community. He had been a good first choice, since if he hadn't been the first, he might have been resentful. As long as he was on board, Mike hoped he could count on Harold and Harry to persuade the other farmers to join in. Maybe they could even help influence Joshua!

It had been a really good day, right from the start. It seemed only fitting to return to the woman that had started it.

*****

When he walked in the door, Liv could see his enthusiasm.

"You look almost too happy. Should I be worried? You didn't meet another woman, did you?" Liv displayed that devilish smile he liked so much. It was this sort of banter that made life with her so much fun, so he played along.

"I can't hide anything from you! Yes, I did meet another woman, but you definitely don't have anything to worry about. She's married, but even if she wasn't, you wouldn't have to worry. I went there to talk to her husband. Harold owns the largest farm in the area, and his son majored in economics. Both of them liked what I proposed!

"If you were talking to farmers, I suppose that means Jake came through!"

"Oh, yeah, he has a semi full of solar panels and accessories. I told him we – you and I –would bring him some contracts to sign tomorrow, so the next phase is up to you. And while you're doing your lawyerly thing, you also need to write a contract for Harry – that's Harold's son. After we get Jake and his boys signed, we need to drop off Harry's contract for him to review."

"Okay, I've drawn up some preliminary stuff based on what we talked about. Do you want to go over them now?"

She had been very thorough. Mike was concerned that some of it contained too much 'legalese', and she agreed to some changes he suggested while insisting that some of it was necessary to ensure that the contracts would 'hold up in court'. Of course, they both knew there weren't any courts, but she was right to make sure these documents would be binding on all parties. She would be the one responsible for settling disputes, and she wanted to be sure there weren't any obvious loop-holes someone could use to get out of fulfilling their responsibilities.

The discussion was sometimes heated, but they compromised until both were satisfied. Throughout the negotiating, neither had lost their cool – or their sense of humor. By the time they were finished, it was dinnertime and Mike said "So, do you feel like cooking, or should I call for a pizza?" Fortunately, Liv felt like cooking.

Chapter 20 – Where there's a will... there's a lawyer

The sun, peeking through the bedroom window, caught Mike's attention. He told himself he didn't have to get up right away, as he closed his eyes and reached toward Liv. She wasn't there. Now he was awake!

"What are you doing up so early?" he asked, when he found her in the walk-in closet.

"I don't know what to wear!"

"Well, Jake's boys haven't been around women for a while, so please wear *something!*"

She wasn't laughing. Apparently, finding the right thing to wear was a major issue, so Mike had better take it seriously. "You are an attorney. I think you should dress professionally. Does that help?"

Of course that didn't help. Of course she would 'dress professionally'. It wasn't her wardrobe that was troubling her. It had been a long time since she'd had to take a leading role in something important. Mike was relying on her to do her part, and she was afraid of failing. Why didn't he understand that? He had dared to face Jake and then the farmer without flinching, but she wasn't as brave as he was. Was he brave or just over-confident? Did it never occur to him that he might not succeed? It must be confidence. She wasn't as confident as he was.

Mike sensed she was nervous about the meeting. It couldn't be a question of what to wear, because she knew how to dress to impress. He had been impressed! "Honey, they will be blown away by your smile *and* your professionalism, no matter what you wear. You'll be fine, I know it – and by the way, I love you."

She took a breath and smiled. He *did* understand!

He jumped in the shower while she finished dressing. *"Damn! That water is cold. It'll be nice when we can have fresh water whenever we want it, so it can pass through the water heater first."*

She was almost ready when he entered the closet. "Well, I guess it doesn't matter what I wear. Nobody's going to notice me standing next to *you!*"

"Thank you, kind sir, but if you're going to stand next to me, you might want to wear a suit instead of your usual leather bomber jacket."

"I'll wear a sport coat and slacks...but no tie! I gotta draw the line somewhere."

When Mike walked into the kitchen, Plato barked once, then stopped and stared inquisitively. Mike was dressed much the way he used to before the blackout, but that was a long time ago and even Plato was surprised.

On the drive out to Jake's, Liv was flipping through the pages of her contracts. Mike didn't want to add to her stress, but she was getting on his nerves. Finally, he said – as softly as he could – "Liv, everything is in order. There's nothing to worry about. They're going to like you, and they're going to sign anything you ask them to sign. Relax, please." She didn't answer, but she put the papers back in her portfolio.

Mike stopped the car and barely had time to honk the horn when Jake and Sam both came out to meet them. "Hi Mike, and you must be Liv. I'm Jake." He was opening the passenger door, with Sam hovering close behind.

"Hello Jake. Who's your friend?"

"I'm Sam, pleased to meet you ma'am."

As they walked to the house, Jake said "Mike, you said she was a lawyer. You didn't tell us she was also a glamour model."

Liv didn't give Mike a chance to answer. "What were you expecting, Jake?"

"I don't know...horn-rimmed glasses...hair in a bun...frumpy..."

"I could wear the glasses and wear my hair up if it would make you feel more comfortable, but I don't do frumpy. Sorry."

"Ha-ha. I can see why you like her, Mike. She's got more than just good looks. Welcome to our humble abode. You've met Sam. This is Martin, and that one over there is Radar. We got a few others around here, but they're out pretending to be farmers. We all gotta eat, you know."

"You can't fool me. Radar is shorter and wears glasses...and he's, you know...frumpy."

Everyone was laughing now, even Radar. She had nothing to worry about. By the time they settled down to discuss the business details, it was as if they had all been friends for a long time.

Mike said "Sam, you might have your first customer by Friday, if you can be ready by then."

"Ready and able!"

The boys wanted to seal the deal with a drink, but Mike had to decline. Their next stop was going to be at the home of their big client, who happened to be Mormon. Mike wasn't going to risk offending him by having alcohol on his breath.

As they drove to Harold's farm, Mike turned to Liv. "You were great, just as I knew you would be. I think you could fit in with any crowd, so I probably don't have to tell you this but our next stop is likely to be less jovial. Harold, Harry and their women don't seem like the jovial type."

Liv said "Gotcha. How's this?" as she put her hair up and fastened the top button of her blouse. Mike almost told her she looked like Jake *thought* she would, but caught himself just in time.

Instead, he said "You look very professional, dear" as they turned into the driveway to Harold's farm.

The ritual of stopping and honking was becoming second-nature now. This time the girls came out without their rifles. That was reassuring. And this time they introduced themselves, although Mike noticed that they were only speaking to Liv. He was beginning to wonder if they were going to invite him in or if they expected him to wait in the car, when Harry walked up to the driver's door and greeted Mike. As Mike followed Harry toward the house, it looked like the girls were taking Liv in another direction. Mike stopped walking and said...

"Harry, Sam assures me he will be open for business by Friday, so I hope we can agree on terms before then. As promised, though, I will leave the paperwork with you for now. You can let me know when you're ready to proceed. Uh, Liv is an attorney, and she came with me because she is better qualified to answer any questions you might have, so if you'd like, the *three* of us can sit down together now."

"Oh, I see. I didn't realize...of course." He shouted in the direction of the departing women "Sisters, the lady is here on business. Perhaps she could visit with you another time." Then, to Mike he said "I apologize for the confusion. We don't get many visitors, and the girls only get to town on Sundays for church. They were thrilled at the opportunity to meet someone new, but of course, I understand now that this was not a social call."

That settled, they sat around the kitchen table to review the paperwork Liv had prepared. Before they had begun, Harold joined them. "I have a question for you, Mike. I understand you will be making us a loan so that we may purchase fuel, and that we are expected to repay that loan by selling our crops. I am an honest businessman. If I promise to do something, I will do it if it is at all possible, but what if I am unable? What if I cannot sell my crops or if inclement weather prevents us from harvesting them?"

"Harold, I understand your concerns. As Harry mentioned the last time we spoke, this is not a textbook economy we are proposing so, let me explain what you will be reading in all these documents. You will be signing a loan commitment for a line of credit, but in order to qualify for a loan you will be joining a merchant's club, for lack of a better term for it. The loan document will look much like any you may have seen before, but it is the terms of the membership that will answer your question. Harry will have time to read all of the legal jargon to confirm that it says what I am saying, but I'm going to give it to you in layman's terms first. And Liv will no doubt correct me if I get any of it wrong."

Mike continued: "When you become a member, you are agreeing to offer products or services for sale to other members. You must be a member to obtain financing. As long as you continuously offer products or services for sale, you are a member in good standing. As a member, your loan repayments will be deducted from your revenue automatically, and your account balance will be increased by your income and decreased by any additional purchases. Anyone you buy from will get paid, even though it may put your account in a deficit. You can carry a deficit indefinitely as long as you continue to be a vendor. Remember, there are no interest charges. So, you cannot default unless you attempt to cancel your membership. Do you understand it so far?"

Harry replied "So we can't cancel our membership until we've satisfied our debt. That's reasonable. I assume we can cancel if we no longer owe anything?"

"Yes, but cancelling would end your ability to buy or sell to other members. There is no cash currency, so without a membership, you would have no way to pay for anything you might want or any way for other members to pay you. Think of it this way: In the US, everyone accepted US dollars, but not Mexican Pesos. If someone wanted to pay you in Pesos, you would not sell to them, nor would anyone sell to you if you only had Pesos to give them."

"I understand why we wouldn't want to cancel, but there must be a point where our debts could exceed some preset limit that would cause *you* to cancel our membership."

"Not as long as you are still acting in good faith as a vendor. By that, I mean you are still trying to sell goods. If business turns sour and you sell nothing at all in a thirty day period, the terms of the membership dictate that we must counsel you - and you must accept our counsel. We might suggest things you could do to increase your sales. If you have no sales for a period of six consecutive months, your membership will terminate and any collateral you provided for the loan can be forfeited. That is a worst-case scenario, and one I hope will never occur, but the condition had to be included to prevent anyone from thinking they could simply walk away with no consequences. Does that seem reasonable to you?"

It was Harold who spoke this time. "That's more than reasonable. A bank would never offer such terms. Not only would they gouge us with interest and late fees, but they'd expect some payment from us every month even if we didn't earn a dime! Still, some might take advantage of you, spending more than they could ever hope to earn. What incentive is there for a man to earn more than he spends?"

"That's a good question! I'm a firm believer in a strong work ethic, and I know not everyone shares that belief. But I am also a firm believer in the power of incentives to encourage people to work. We've talked about the worst-case scenario, but now let's talk about the best case. If your business is successful and you spend less than you earn, you could repay your loan and enjoy a substantial credit balance. That would mean you could take a vacation, or even retire someday, knowing you had a nest-egg to support you when you are no longer working. Your membership can't be cancelled by us as long as you have a credit balance."

Harry chimed in "That's a relief. Initially, I thought you were a Capitalist, but you were beginning to sound like a Socialist.

Apparently, you've blended the best of both. Still, if you are a Capitalist, how can you afford to do this?"

"Our only income is 4% of every transaction, paid by the seller – much like Visa charged merchants for the privilege of accepting a credit card. If you're not making sales, we aren't earning anything. We really are in this together. This would never work on a global or even a national scale, but I believe it can work in a community our size. I hope you think so, too."

"Mike, I think you know by now, we're members of the LDS church. We have always considered our Church to be our community. You're asking us to become part of a larger community. Because of our experience with you so far, I find it easy to trust you but it is going to be difficult to persuade others to welcome outsiders. I apologize if that sounds rude, but there are some in this town - what you are calling the 'community' - that have not been friendly to us in the past."

"Harold, in the past we had the luxury of ignoring our neighbors. I was as guilty of that as anyone. I hardly knew the people on my own street, but lately I have reached out to people I never knew existed. There are not many of us, and I believe we need each other. We should not allow our past differences to stop us from working together. It might not surprise you to learn that Jake expressed feelings very similar to your own, but he is ready to work with you – or at least to trade with you – and I believe he will do so honorably. Just don't expect him to join your Church."

"Heh-heh, I don't expect to persuade him. I'll leave that task to the Lord, although I doubt even He could do it. Harry will still need to read your contracts before we'll sign, but I appreciate you taking the time to explain it. It sounds good to me. Tell me where you live, and we'll bring the documents to you Thursday afternoon."

"Thank you for listening. I look forward to a long and successful relationship."

On the way home, Liv said "You're a damn good salesman. You could charm the pants off anyone!"

"I'm glad you think so, because I was just thinking about charming the pants off *you* as soon as we get home."

Chapter 21 – The Waiting Game

There wasn't much to do until Thursday, and then only if Harold showed up as promised. Mike was antsy, and getting on Liv's nerves. She wasn't sure if this was the right time to raise this issue, but she was tired of showering in the Master bath, and then going to the guest bath to apply her makeup. Mike had insisted she move her clothes into the Master closet, but sharing a bathroom hadn't been discussed. It was silly, but little things like that had a tendency to define the stages of a relationship, and theirs wasn't quite as far along as she thought it should be.

"Honey, do you think there's room in the Master bath for some of my things?"

Mike was just staring. She didn't know what that meant, but a simple 'yes' would have been nice. What was keeping him from this last little commitment?

"Of course, I didn't realize you were still using the guest bath. Move your stuff, but...I don't mind sharing the room, but I have a thing about sharing drawers. I hope you don't think it's weird, but I don't want to have to rummage through your stuff to find my stuff. Can you live with that?"

She was so relieved, she couldn't think of a response – except to kiss him. While she rearranged her toiletries, Mike picked up a book. Liv thought *"Good, he found something to distract himself. Maybe he would stop pacing!"*

Mike was pleased with the progress they had made with Jake and Harry, but there was so much more that needed to change! He was plotting his next move when Liv asked something about the bathroom. *"What was she talking about? Oh, yeah, she's 'nesting'. She wants to know she belongs here – that he wanted her to be here. Couldn't she tell how much he cared for her? Why do women need constant reassurance?"* Well, there was no point in wondering. He was never going to understand women, but he really loved *this* woman, so he gave her what she seemed to need.

That distraction was probably just what he needed. There was no point in any more planning yet. Things take time. To keep himself from thinking, he selected a book from the shelf and tried to get interested in it.

Later, they played Monopoly. He hadn't played in years. It was a nice way to pass the time. They were evenly matched, so the game went on and on. Liv had the better real estate, like 'Park Place' but Mike had the railroads and the 'Electric Company'. He hoped it wasn't an omen, but neither of them got the chance to buy the 'Water Works'.

Chapter 22 – Politics

Mike woke early Thursday morning. Harold wasn't due until the afternoon, but Mike was too wired to sleep. He had been thinking about ways to structure the 'water company' as he had come to think of it. Should it be privately owned, and therefore privately managed, or should it belong to the community – sort of a municipal entity. Mike felt they had done nicely without any form of government, so he was reluctant to create a bureaucracy. He'd have to talk with Liv. It's good to have a 'sounding board' if for no other reason than to hear your own thoughts out loud, but he also respected her opinions.

He was anxious to have that conversation, but reluctant to wake her. She looked even more beautiful when she was sleeping. So, he lay back quietly and watched her sleep.

When she finally stirred, Mike pretended to be asleep. He enjoyed watching her, but he felt a little like a stalker! It would be better if she didn't know about his little perversion. As she moved more, Mike pretended to wake up for the first time.

"I'm sorry, did I wake you?"

"Not a problem, if you're up I want to be, too. In case I've never mentioned it, I like spending time with you."

Liv thought *"Yup, he's a salesman alright."* But she loved him anyway.

Mike waited until they had finished breakfast before bringing up the subject that had interfered with his sleep. "Liv, I'd like your opinion on something."

"Sure, what is it?"

"I've been thinking about the water treatment operation. As long as the Bishop thinks it's his to do with as he sees fit, I'm afraid it will never reach its full potential. But I can't decide if it should become a private company or if it should belong to the community at large. What do you think?"

"Hmm, I hadn't thought about it. I'd like to give it more thought, but off the top of my head I see a problem with privatizing it. We don't want anyone to have the power to deny water to anyone, do we?"

"That's a good point. I believe in private enterprise, but too much control in the hands of a few has its risks. On the other hand, I don't like the idea of creating a government bureaucracy. I never thought of myself as an anarchist before, but the longer we survive without a government, the more I think we really don't need one."

"Yes, there are pros and cons to both ideas. Maybe what is needed is a third option. I don't know what that might be, but maybe we should think more about it. I will if you will!"

"You're right. Most of the time, we're encouraged to choose between two options, but there's usually more than two. We just have to look beyond the obvious to find them. Thanks, I'll give it some more thought, too."

Mike stepped outside for a cigarette. Plato joined him, as usual. The dog didn't seem to mind the smoke, but Liv wasn't a smoker, and she didn't approve of his habit. She knew she wasn't going to change him, but she also knew she wouldn't have to. His supply was dwindling, and he was down to two smokes a day. She could tolerate it twice a day as long as he smoked outside – and didn't try to kiss her until he'd had something to eat or drink.

They both found books of interest and read until they got hungry. They were just finishing a light lunch when there was a knock on the door. Plato got to the door first, but waited for Mike to tell him if the visitors were 'friend or foe'. Harold and Harry had brought a third man with them.

"Hello Mike, I hope this is a convenient time?"

"Yes, please come in Harold. Hello, Harry and…I don't believe we've met. "

"This is my friend and neighbor, Winston. He owns the farm next to mine, I've been telling him of your plans, and I hope you don't mind, but he would like to be a part of this enterprise as well."

"I'm pleased to hear that. This is Plato, our 'Sergeant-at-arms'. He won't bite. He just needs assurance that you are no threat. And this is Liv. If you want to join us, Winston, Liv will need some information from you in order to prepare a contract. Let's sit in the living room."

Liv offered the guests some water. She and Mike were drinking coffee, but she knew they weren't coffee drinkers, and there wasn't anything else available.

Mike gave Winston a brief recap of the membership concept just to be sure he had heard enough from Harold to make an informed decision. Winston was enthused. Liv took a few notes and excused herself to prepare the paperwork needed for their new member.

Harold looked like he had something on his mind, and Mike was afraid he was having second thoughts. "Harold, is there something you'd like to talk about?"

"Yes Mike, you mentioned the possibility of getting us more water, and you alluded to Joshua as a 'stumbling block' – I think that was the term you used. I assume you have discussed your ideas with him?"

"We did have a long chat the day he informed me that my services were no longer needed at the plant. Wait. That came out wrong. I *was* finished at the plant. Jonathon is a very capable engineer, and I am confident that he can handle the day-to-day operations there without my help. In fact, I had suggested letting *most* of the men go, but the Bishop wanted all of them to stay. I got the impression he felt I was the only person who was dispensable. But he explained his motivation quite adequately. He sees it necessary to keep the men employed to justify feeding them. I sympathize with his predicament, but we have...shall we say, 'philosophical differences' when it comes to how best to keep people gainfully employed."

It was Winston who continued the questioning. "But in your conversation with Joshua, did you offer suggestions as to how we could increase the output of the plant and how we could all acquire fuel for our tractors?"

"Yes, we discussed most of what Harry and I talked about the other day. The idea didn't appeal to him."

"This is troubling."

That comment was directed toward Harold, not Mike, but Mike felt it necessary to speak. "Listen, I'm not trying to cause friction in your Church. He is your Bishop, and I understand why it is necessary for you to comply with his wishes. Please don't do anything rash because of me!"

Harold and Winston were both smiling, but Harry couldn't hold back a hearty laugh. Mike was confused.

Harold explained "Mike, I forgot you are not LDS. The Bishop is a servant in the Church, not its leader."

"But...Look, you're right. I don't know much about your church's hierarchy. I was raised Catholic, and a layman doesn't tell a Bishop what to do. That would be like an army Colonel taking orders from a civilian."

They all got a laugh out of that.

"What am I missing here? Let me in on the joke."

"A Bishop is appointed to manage a Ward for a two-year term. It is normally a low-level management position where he answers to the person in charge of a larger group called a Stake. Well, that's not important. All you need to know is that all of the mid-level managers serve at the pleasure of the Elders."

"Wait a minute. The Elders...you're talking about Joseph Smith and Brigham Young. Maybe you think you are still communicating with them but I'm pretty sure they are dead."

"No, Mike you have named the Prophets, and yes, they have passed but I assure you the Elders are very much alive. I should know. I am one of them, and so is Winston here. I see your confusion stems from your military experience and your Catholic upbringing. Perhaps this analogy will serve you better. Even if the Bishop was a CEO – he would still answer to the Board of

Directors. You may think of the Elders as the Board of Directors of the LDS Church. That's also not entirely accurate, but much closer to the truth than what you were thinking."

"I feel terrible! By talking to you, I've gone over Joshua's head. That wasn't my intention, exactly, but he's not going to be happy."

Winston wasn't going to give Joshua any sympathy. "That is his fault, not yours. He had a responsibility to inform us of any options that might be available, regardless of his opinion of them. Because of the unusual situation the blackout has caused, we have given him much more latitude than his position warrants, but this was not his decision to make."

"That's true." Harold agreed with Winston. "I am grateful that you approached us, Mike, otherwise we would have known nothing of this opportunity."

Liv had completed the necessary contracts and joined them just as Harold was expressing his gratitude. She replied "We are grateful you had the wisdom to see the benefits of the opportunity. I have a few documents that require your signatures. Let's take a few minutes to review them one by one, shall we gentlemen?"

Once the papers were signed, Mike wanted to celebrate alone with Liv, but no one was making an effort to leave! Finally, Harold spoke up. "Mike, this is just the first step in your plan. I would like to discuss your ideas for expanding the productivity of the water plant. We would be pleased if you would assume control of the plant. I assure you, there will be no 'stumbling block' in your path."

"Thank you, but I have no desire to run the plant. Just this morning Liv and I were discussing the various ways the plant could be owned, and after talking with you this afternoon, I would suggest everyone in the community become a stock holder in the venture. And, like most corporations, management decisions would be made by a Board of Directors. I think I can persuade everyone in our community to appoint the Elders as that Board – initially. Understand, though, that at some reasonable interval elections should be held to determine if any of the Board Members should be changed. If all goes smoothly, no changes are likely. People rarely vote for change if they are happy with the status quo. I would also strongly recommend you give some thought to finding a plant manager. Jonathon is a good engineer, but he hasn't demonstrated much in the way of personnel management qualities. My role, as I see it, would be as a consultant during the expansion. "

"You do not want a permanent management role?"

"No. I see it this way: I'm sure you know that it takes both fuel and oxygen to make a fire, but large quantities of both – even if combined – will not produce a fire. For that, a spark is needed. I look around our community and I see an abundance of potential – oxygen and fuel, so to speak. I think the best contribution I can make is to be the spark."

"Very well, Mike. I will call a meeting of the Elders for Saturday. I would like you to explain your ideas to all of us. Can you be at the church at 10AM?"

"Sure. I'd like Liv to accompany me, in case any legal questions arise – that's her domain."

"That is acceptable. Joshua will be there, as well. I insist on that,

Mike. He needs to learn from this experience."

That was settled. Mike told the men where Sam's Gas station was located. They assured him they would be visiting Sam tomorrow.

Chapter 23 – Putting the Pieces Together

Now that there were customers for the gas station, Mike needed to make sure Sam would be ready. It sure would be nice if they had phone service. That was going to be next on his list. Mike figured if he was going to have to drive out to talk to Sam, he might as well talk with Radar while he was there.

It was mid-afternoon. There was plenty of time to check in with Sam. Liv said she'd prefer to stay home, so Mike took Plato for company. Plato never refused a chance to go for a ride, and Mike realized it had been a long time since he'd been able to take his furry friend along.

Jake was glad to see Mike and almost as happy to meet Plato. It was a while before Mike could steer the conversation toward business.

Finally, Jake said "Hey, I'm glad you're here. We've been taking inventory, and we have even more potential than I thought. There are 150 completed panels and enough materials to build another 300 at least. We've also got 80 power inverters and gobs of wire. The only thing we're a little short on is batteries."

"When I first ventured out, I stood on the freeway overpass and looked down on a sea of abandoned vehicles. There's a battery in every one of those cars and trucks! They're not the best kind of batteries for a solar installation, but they'll have to do. It'll be time-consuming pulling them all out, but I don't think we'll run out of batteries any time soon. The hardest part will be matching them up so each installation has the same capacity batteries."

"We'll get started on that after we've used up the ones we've got."

"How's Sam coming with the gas station? I've got two farmers signed up, and they're going to be at his place tomorrow looking to buy fuel. I hope he's ready!"

"Yup, we finished the install yesterday. He's over there setting up the bays so he can offer repair service, but there's two pumps set up, one unleaded and one diesel. They're not self-service, though. Sam will have to turn a pump on, pump the fuel, and then lock it back up."

"Wow! I can't remember the last time I saw a full-service gas station! Will he clean the windshield and check the oil, too?"

"Ha-ha, probably not for you, but he might if Liv is driving. Sam is really into this, though. He says he always wanted to own his own repair shop. The rest of my guys are happier working for me, installing solar power systems. I know you said that business would belong to all of us, but Sam's got his own gig and the other guys told me I am their boss, so the solar business is mine and they'll be my employees. Is that okay with you?"

"Sure, you'll want to talk with Liv about writing up some kind of employment contracts. We'll set up accounts for each of them, and their wages will be deducted from your account. You'll have to tell us what you want to pay them and they'll each have a debit card, so they can buy from other merchants."

"Cool, you're even going to handle my payroll for me! I hate paperwork!"

"Yup, we're a full-service...uh...whatever we are. We're not a bank, but something like that. What about Radar? I asked him to think about setting up phone service. Has he given any thought to that?"

"He's out back. I can get him for you, but I know he considered it and he told me it would take a programmer to make everyone's phone work on one network. That's not something he knows how to do, so you're going to have to find somebody else. Sorry."

"That's too bad. I'd really like to get the phones working. Having to drive everywhere to talk to people might be good for Sam's business, but it's a pain in the ass for me."

"Mike, I offered you a drink last time you were here. I understand why you turned it down then, but let's drink a toast today to our mutual success. You've found a way to get us and the Mormons to cooperate. You've really earned a drink!"

"We all have."

*****

Driving home, Mike was grateful there was no traffic. He was even more grateful there were no cops on the road.

Mike was bursting to tell Liv the news. "The gas station is open!"

Liv could smell the alcohol on his breath. "Did you sample it? It smells like a pretty high octane."

"Oh, Jake was disappointed that we didn't drink with them last time, so I had to join him in a toast...or two. It's been a long time since I've taken a drink. I may be a little tipsy."

"Well, as long as you don't tell me you've funded someone to open a bar."

"Ha-ha, in a predominantly Mormon town? That would not be a profitable venture. I did get a disappointment though. Apparently Radar doesn't have the skills to set up a phone system - or the inclination to start a business of any kind. I need to review those notes you gave me to see if any of the unemployed men might have what it takes."

"I don't think you'll find anything in my notes. I'm going to visit Sandra tomorrow. I'm sure she knows more people than I do. I'll ask her."

"Thanks!"

Chapter 24 – Sandra

On Friday morning, Mike didn't bother to get up when Liv dressed for her visit with Sandra. Liv was a little concerned with his mood swings, lately. He would get very enthusiastic when something went as planned, and then mope around when there was nothing happening. She shared his enthusiasm during the good times, but didn't know what to do when he was down. In her business – in her previous life – cases took months, even years to settle. She was accustomed to waiting. Apparently, Mike was not. She wondered what he would be like when, or if, he ran out of projects. Well, that wouldn't happen anytime soon, so she put it out of her mind for now.

Sandra looked surprised as she opened the door. "Liv, I wasn't sure if you would come, considering what's happened."

"What do you mean? I have been looking forward to spend the day together! I don't know why you would think I wouldn't come. What has happened, I don't understand."

Sandra was nearly in tears as she blurted out "Mike has been so mean! How could he go to the Elders behind Joshua's back! Now Josh is in trouble and it's all Mike's fault. I thought you were my friend!"

"Sandra, it wasn't like that. Mike didn't know who the Elders were, or that talking to some farmers would get Joshua in trouble. He is just trying to help all of us. The farmers need fuel for their tractors in order to produce enough to feed us all, and Mike found a way to get them that fuel. He wasn't trying to get Joshua in trouble. He was trying to solve a problem. That's just what Mike does. When he sees a problem, he doesn't rest until he's solved it.

Please, Sandra, you have to understand it wasn't personal!"

"I know it's going to help the farmers and all of us, but Mike should have gone to the Bishop with his ideas."

"Sandra, I don't know what Joshua has told you but...Mike *did* talk to him first."

"You're...you're just taking Mike's side!"

"Sandra, they talked about it in our house. I was there. Mike was very disappointed that Joshua turned Mike's ideas down flat. It was the next day that Mike decided to talk to Harold because he has a large farm and a lot of machinery sitting idle. Mike was afraid Harold would turn him down, too, because we thought the Bishop made all the decisions for everyone in your church. We were pleasantly surprised when Harold, or actually Harry, agreed. It wasn't until a few days later that Harold explained that he was one of the Elders, and how your Church is structured. We didn't know, honest!"

"Joshua wouldn't refuse to help the Elders. That's nonsense. You're talking nonsense."

"Joshua is lucky to have such a loyal friend as you, Sandra, but he ought to be honest with you. If he is in trouble, it is because he didn't relay Mike's ideas to the Elders. Harold said the decision was not Joshua's to make, and I think you know that to be true. More importantly, I hope this doesn't come between *us!* Can we still be friends?"

Sandra was silent for several minutes. "I'm not sure. Maybe someday, but right now I think you should go."

"Okay, I'll go if that's what you want. I hope we can talk again sometime."

Liv resisted the temptation to blame Mike. It really wasn't his fault, but she was fond of Sandra, and this hurt. If Mike hadn't been so adamant about changing things, Sandra would still be her friend. Liv was still debating with herself when she walked into the house.

"You're back early. Is everything okay? I didn't expect to see you so soon."

"Mike, you've ruined everything! Joshua is in serious trouble with the Elders and Sandra won't talk to me! Do you ever think about what your actions will do to other people?"

Mike was stunned. Liv was very upset, and she was blaming him for...*what?*

"What do you want from me, Liv? I've been trying to improve our lives. And not just ours - everyone in town will benefit from the business arrangements we've set up – even Sandra, whether she knows it or not. Would you have me ignore the needs of everyone just so your surrogate daughter will like you?" That was harsh. He knew he'd gone too far, but words can't be retracted once they've been uttered, no matter how much we regret them.

Liv was crying. He didn't know what to say to make any of this better. In situations like this, most men would retreat to the nearest bar. It must be instinct, because Mike didn't have to think about it. He went to Jake's.

"How could he be so cruel?" Liv was talking to Plato, who was gracious enough to listen to anyone who needed to be heard. "I thought I knew him! He's not the man I thought he was. A better man would have stayed here and talked this out calmly and rationally, but he just...left! He says he loves me, but he doesn't care about my feelings!" Her *feelings*. What had come over her? When did she become this emotional wreck? She had always managed to remain emotionally detached while handling all sorts of legal matters that had other people in a frenzy. She was the cool one. *Was.* How did people deal with these sorts of irrational feelings? How could she expect him to discuss it calmly and rationally when she was neither calm nor rational? It was a good thing he left. She didn't want him to see her like this.

"Get a grip, girl! You're better than this!" Plato neither agreed nor disagreed.

But she couldn't 'get a grip'. The more she tried to calm down, the more upset she became, wavering between blaming Mike and defending him. Finally, she had to confront the comment that had hurt the most. Had she been using Sandra as a surrogate for the children she couldn't have?

It was late, and Mike was still not home. Would he ever return? Of course he would – this was his house. Should she leave? Where would she go? She finally decided to go to bed. Oh, no! She couldn't sleep with him until this was sorted out. She decided the only prudent thing would be to move back to the guest room.

It was dark when Mike finally returned home. He had put it off as long as he could. His liver probably couldn't take any more punishment, and he really needed to sleep this off. Maybe she'd be asleep by now. He'd slip in quietly and...what if she said something, or worse, what if she was still crying? The lights were off. He didn't dare turn them on, but slipping in quietly was proving to be difficult in the dark. Okay, he'd have to risk using the little flashlight attached to his key ring. He found the stairs and managed to reach the landing without falling. The guest room door was closed. Was it closed before? He didn't think so. His bed was still made. She wasn't in it. Mike was both relieved and saddened by that.

Chapter 25 – The Elders

As the sun slipped in through the crack between the curtains, Mike, half awake, reached for Liv. The empty bed reminded him of the previous day. His head hurt, which forced him to remember the previous night. Neither memory pleased him.

He showered, shaved and dressed quickly, anxious for a cup of coffee to wash away the cotton in his mouth. The guest room door was still closed, but that didn't mean she wasn't already downstairs. Once he reached the kitchen, he knew he and Plato were the only creatures stirring. Was she still upstairs, or was she even in the house? He looked in the garage. The BMW was still there. Well, she hadn't left him. That was something. Maybe they could still work things out. He really didn't want to lose her.

The meeting with the Elders was set for 10AM. Now would not be a good time to have a long talk with Liv, so maybe it was good that she wasn't up. He needed to prepare himself for the meeting. Public speaking was not his favorite pastime. Talking with one or a couple of people was fine, but addressing a Board of Directors meeting always scared him. Well, at least he wasn't going to face them alone. He had insisted they include Liv in the meeting. Oh, shit! He *was* going to have to talk to her this morning, and fast.

He knocked softly on the bedroom door. "Liv, are you awake?"

"Yes."

"Honey, I'm sorry for yesterday. Can we talk about it?"

"I don't want to talk about it."

"Well, okay. Will you come down and have some coffee?"

"Not right now, maybe later."

"Uh, the meeting is at 10, so I thought you'd like to grab a cup before we have to leave."

"I'm not going."

Great! He'd not only lost his lover, he'd also lost his business partner.

At 9:45 Mike gave up any hope of having Liv by his side. It was time to go. It was going to take all his willpower to keep from punching Joshua in front of the Elders.

"Watch over Liv while I'm gone, Plato. I'm counting on you."

It was a good thing there was no traffic, because Mike had to break a few speeding laws to get to the church on time.

As he walked into the church, his worst fears were realized. They had arranged several tables in a semi-circle, and the Elders were seated behind them. There was one chair in front of the tables, facing the group. It was a safe assumption they expected him to sit in that chair. One chair, not two. Even if Liv had come with him as planned, they had seen to it that he would have to confront them alone.

He sat in the chair, not because he wanted to but because his legs were starting to give out. Liv would have had no problem in a situation like this. The old Liv, that is. He didn't understand the Liv he'd seen yesterday.

Harold called out "Mike thanks for joining us. Please sit here next to me. *That* chair is for Joshua." He continued, but Mike almost missed what he was saying. "We also have a chair here for

Liv. I understood she would be joining us as well."

"Oh, uh, she's feeling a bit under the weather." Then he hastily added "She sends her regrets."

"I hope she recovers quickly. Well, shall we begin? Winston, please escort Joshua to his seat."

Once Joshua was seated, Harold continued. "Mike, we are all anxious to avail ourselves of your generous offer to extend us credit to purchase fuel for our tractors. I do not wish to minimize our gratitude for what you have done, or for the assistance you provided in getting the water turned on, but today we want to hear your plans for expanding the water output."

"Very well, first let me say that Jonathon has seen to the conversion from automation to a more mechanical operation at the plant. It has the capability to serve our needs. The only thing lacking is power to run the pumps. The two generators are insufficient, and they use a lot of liquid fuel – something we don't have in abundance. I propose the installation of a large solar array to run the pumps with electricity. Between the solar panels and an equally large bank of batteries, it will be possible to increase the water pressure and to maintain that pressure twenty-four hours a day."

There was no dissension so far, so Mike continued. "Such an installation cannot be accomplished for free. The water plant must generate more than water. It must also generate revenue to pay for the upgrade. In my opinion, it should also be put in a position to be able to pay wages to those who keep it running. To accomplish that, I propose giving every member of the community a share in the ownership of the plant, and establishing a Board of Directors to oversee its continued operation. Initially, the Elders will serve as the Directors, but eventually, it will be up to the shareholders to either reelect you or replace you. The water company would then be treated as a merchant, entitled to a line of credit sufficient to pay for the upgrades. But to be a merchant, it must have a reasonable expectation of repaying the loan. Therefore, every water consumer must be expected to pay for what they receive."

After some mumbling among the Elders, and Winston was the first to verbalize their concerns. "That will not be a problem for those of us who are merchants, but how will others pay their water bills?"

"Ultimately, we need to find a way to reach full employment, but that won't happen overnight. In the meantime, I will ask the Church to pay the bills for its members that have no income source yet. Historically, it has been the churches that have seen to the needs of the indigent. Churches have done so since before there were governments. The Roman Catholic Church kept people alive through the Dark Ages when government consisted of war lords who did not have the best interests of their citizens in mind. Muslims have fed people in war-torn countries for centuries. You have been feeding your people, why wouldn't you also provide them with water? For that matter, I would like to see the Church pay the farmers for the food you have been distributing."

Another of the Elders was shaking his head. "You have me confused. The Church is not a merchant. How can it pay for anything?"

"I don't claim to be too knowledgeable about the doctrines of your faith, but I believe you ask all of your flock to tithe. Surely, the merchants who are LDS will give the Church a percentage of the credits they earn from their businesses. The Church will not be a merchant, but it will have a source of income and its own debit card, much the same as employees of the water plant will. With their wages, they will be able to buy from merchants. They will also be able to pay their own water bills. I'm asking the Church to subsidize those who are neither merchants nor gainfully employed – yet."

Harold was laughing. "And, no doubt, you have plans to ensure employment for everyone."

"I can't guarantee full employment. I'm not going to put a gun to anyone's head and force them to work. But together we can help create opportunities for those who are willing to take them. Those who aren't merchants will always be dependent upon those who are – either as recipients of welfare or as useful employees. Given the choice, I believe most people would choose to be useful. To start, Jonathon is a good engineer as I have mentioned several times, His expertise was vital in the early stages of our task. But he is not a manager. The Board will have to select someone with the qualifications needed. Jonathon should be employed as the chief engineer, but there is a need for many qualified people to man the plant if we are to keep it open 24/7."

Throughout this discussion, Joshua had sat obediently silent, but his fidgeting was becoming difficult to ignore. Finally, Harold acknowledged Joshua's discomfort. "We have tortured our young Bishop long enough. Joshua, you may speak."

"The more I hear of Mike's plan, the more I realize the wisdom of my decision to not inform the Elders. Don't you see he is taking control of us! Control that rightfully belongs to this Council! He has tempted you with water and then with fuel, but he will be returning us all to the evils of Capitalism if you don't stop him. This grand plan of his will create two classes of people, merchants and peons. You may think it wise, since you are the merchants, but I beg of you - think of the degradation it will cause for the others!"

"May I address Joshua's allegations, Harold?"

"Please do!"

"I understand you received your degree in Political Science. It's obvious your professors were fond of Marx and Lenin but leery of the Capitalist system that afforded them the luxurious life they enjoyed. That's not surprising. Some in academia have little or no experience in - or knowledge of - the real world about which they teach."

Mike glanced around and saw several smiles. Turning back to face Joshua, he continued. "What do you think most people would find more degrading, working for a living or being completely dependent upon the good graces of their neighbors? Before you answer, let me clarify something that seems to be the cause of your misunderstanding. Many years ago, when Marx was writing his scathing expose on Capitalism, working conditions were pretty poor for most workers. That was hardly the case in modern times, and yet many felt like indentured servants – slaves to their jobs. Only it wasn't the fault of their employers! It was due to their own greed."

Mike paused, knowing people would probably disagree.

"Now just a minute... You're saying everyone was greedy?" It was Winston who spoke up. Mike figured it would have been Joshua, but either way it gave him the opening he wanted to explain his claim.

"With the advent of easy credit, most people borrowed such enormous sums of money to satisfy their *wants* – not just their needs – that they became slaves to their own debt. Paying only the minimum required, combined with outrageous interest rates, left them with little hope of ever procuring their freedom. Their choices of employment rarely had anything to do with what they might enjoy and everything to do with what would pay enough to service their debt. So, they were miserable. Not surprisingly, many blamed their employers rather than blaming themselves. We are extending credit to merchants, but not to others, so as to prevent the thing that caused so many so much grief."

"If debt is so bad, why do you offer practically unlimited credit to merchants? By doing so, you are creating a privileged class!" Joshua just couldn't get past his socialist education.

"There will not be two classes of people, but there *are* two classes of debt. When a person borrows to create or expand a business, the money multiplies by creating jobs. It is money invested in something that may have a long-term benefit for many people. When the money is borrowed only to be spent on short-term luxuries, it doesn't have a lasting effect. The only thing that lasts is the debt. Granted, consumption creates jobs, but not nearly as many jobs as the building of a business can."

Once again, it was Joshua who replied. "But you are condemning most people to a lifetime of poverty! If no credit is available, how can they afford..."

Mike finished Joshua's thought for him. "A house? A car? Credit was necessary for major purchases, but no one here needs to buy a house or a car. None of us have mortgages anymore, and no one will need one for a long time to come. But people used credit for everyday expenses. And that's what got many people in trouble. No one will be in debt unless they finance a business that has a good chance of improving their finances – not ruining their finances."

Mike looked at Joshua, expecting another objection, but Joshua was silent so Mike continued.

"They may not have taught you this in school, but in a closed economy, building a business increases wealth and lifts all boats. Capitalism worked well in the US until we expanded our trade with other nations. In a global marketplace, the consumer may purchase something made in another country, thus contributing to *that* countries economy, while removing wealth from his own. We, through no real effort of our own, find ourselves in a closed economy now. Every credit earned and every credit spent will stay in our community, and we will all benefit. But I don't want to see the ruination that personal debt has created in the past. Businesses may take on debt because they are using it to generate the means to repay the loan. Individuals take on debt only to consume it, so we will not extend credit to individuals."

Not surprisingly, Joshua still couldn't accept that. "That's a fine speech, but it doesn't change the fact that some people will have to perform menial tasks just to survive. And the employers will benefit more from the worker's labor than the worker will."

"Possibly. That depends on what you define as a benefit. Providing for one's family should be a reason for pride. It can restore one's dignity - something charity cannot do. Everyone wants to feel needed and useful in some way or another. Work, for many, fills that need. Besides, anyone can be a merchant. We just have to open our imaginations to the possibilities. Some people claim Capitalism is ruled by greed, but self-interest is a natural human trait. Most successful capitalists learn that the best way to become wealthy is to provide things other people want, and are willing to pay for. Capitalism improves the lives of both buyers and sellers while encouraging innovation that Socialism fails to promote".

Mike continued "I've heard that Winston's wife makes a berry pie that is out of this world. Is that true?" Everyone had something good to say about her pies. "I imagine most people would be willing to pay a small price for the privilege of taking one of her pies home. She could be a merchant, if she were so inclined. Some of us like to cook, but others would prefer to pay someone to cook for them. This town could use a restaurant or two." That idea seemed to be popular, too.

Then Mike made his final pitch "In a community as small as ours, it is important for all of us that everyone contributes in some way. This will be especially important in the future, and I hope all of you will join me in persuading our teenagers to seek apprenticeships with those who have useful skills - not only for the benefit of the employers, but for the benefit of the youths. What will they do when we're gone, if they don't learn from us while we're here?"

Another of the Elders – Mike couldn't remember all of their names – stood up and said "That is something I strongly support! We have grown accustomed to sending our children off to college, expecting others to teach them something useful. Joshua, through no fault of his own, is an example of what was wrong with that approach. It is time we took responsibility for educating our children in the ways we believe to be correct. We have always done that regarding our religious beliefs but there are other matters that are also important if they are to live lives worthy of our Lord's blessings."

Harold took the floor. "We have heard enough. Now we must deliberate. Mike, I must ask you and Joshua to leave us now. Please wait outside. We will call for you when we have reached a decision."

As soon as the doors had closed behind them, Joshua began his tirade. "You had no right to speak to me or about me in that way! I helped you when you came to me in need. I offered you a chance to be useful and this is how you repay me?"

Mike had heard enough. "You pompous ass! I have more than repaid any kindness you extended to me and to Liv." Thinking about Liv, Mike continued. "And you didn't have the guts to level with your cousin. Sandra and Liv had grown fond of each other, and you turned Sandra against me and against Liv. Liv is devastated! You've managed to ruin my personal life, but I will not let you ruin things for everyone else in this town!"

"You went behind my back! That was a devious ploy!"

"I didn't know I was going behind your back! I didn't know you had to answer to a bunch of farmers. I thought *you* were *their* leader! If you want to blame me, blame me for being ignorant, but not devious."

Although Joshua's face was still red with anger, he couldn't keep from laughing.

"What's so funny?"

"The idea that your ignorance of LDS has been the cause of my discomfort. It is your ignorance of history that is the real problem."

"History? You mean the biased version you were taught? Communism has failed everywhere it has been tried. Capitalism allowed this nation to achieve greatness, once. The problems we've faced in recent years were not caused by Capitalism, but by consumerism. An economy based upon debt is destined to fail. History also shows us *that*."

The argument would have continued until one or the other dropped from exhaustion, but they were summoned to return to the church. The Council of Elders had reached a decision.

"Mike, again I want to express our thanks for all that you have done. We are in agreement with you on the plans you have offered today. We have decided to grant you the authority to carry out those plans as Mayor of our town."

Mike was stunned. What the hell were they thinking? They were trying to set up a government and, even worse, *they wanted to make him a bureaucrat!* It took a few moments for him to form a response.

"Gentlemen, I am pleased that you agree with my vision for our town's future and honored that you would bestow such a lofty title upon me, but we don't need to establish a government. The purpose of government is to do those things that can't be accomplished by individuals working together voluntarily. We seem to have voluntarily agreed to do the things that need to be done, so there is no need for a government – consequently, we do not need a Mayor."

Harold looked disappointed. This Mayor thing must have been

his idea.

"But, I'm not sure we can accomplish everything that needs to be done without some civil authority. We appreciate your asking us to serve as the Board of Directors for the water treatment plant, but we are concerned that those in the community that are not LDS might think we have established a theocracy!"

Mike hadn't considered that. "That is a valid point that only serves to demonstrate the wisdom of this Council. Appearances are important. Rather than appoint the Elders to the Board, let's list your individual names on a ballot, and put the decision up for a vote of all the shareholders. You are respected members of the community in your own rights, regardless of your positions in the Church. To further dispel the notion that the Church alone will be running the plant, I'll add my name and Jake's to the ballot. Then, we'll let the people select five of us for the Board seats. How does that sound?"

After a brief consultation, the idea was approved.

"As to your concern that we might have other needs, I actually agree. I am considering setting up a volunteer fire department. Since it would be staffed by volunteers, it still doesn't require government oversight. A fire department usually includes emergency responders. I know Sandra has had some medical training. Who else among us would qualify?"

"We have a pediatrician and a surgeon in our Ward. Joshua, you will speak to them about this - and report back to us, please. Is there anything else?"

"Yes, I had hopes of reporting some progress on this, but I haven't gotten very far. I would like to get local telephone service up and running. There are several cell towers in and around town. Jake's boys can provide power to them, but as I understand it we need a computer programmer to design a network suitable for our needs. I don't envision anyone streaming videos, just the ability to talk and maybe text would be nice. Do you know anyone with knowledge in that area?"

"I can't think of anyone off-hand, but I know little about such things. We will ask after church services on Sunday. If we find anyone that might be able to help, I'll have that person contact you. I think we have accomplished enough for one day. We are adjourned."

Chapter 26 – Mending fences

All in all, the meeting was a success. Before going home, Mike thought it would be a good idea to fill Jake in on what had been decided – especially since Jake would be on the ballot for a seat on the Board. This time, Mike would politely refuse any offers that included alcohol. His head still hurt!

Jake wasn't enthusiastic about the possibility of having a hand in managing the water company. He was still leery of the Mormons because of their mutual history. Apparently, Jake's family was there first, before the Mormons settled in the valley. There had been battles over property lines or some such thing, and the bad blood continued for generations. When Jake's father died, none of his Mormon neighbors attended the funeral. Jake took over the family farm after his last tour of duty and inherited the family feud.

At least he was willing to work with them as long as he could do so as an equal – as the owner/manager of a business with products and services they needed – but he saw being on the Board a step in the wrong direction. They would have to debate and compromise on too many issues, and he would be outnumbered. Jake wanted Mike on the Board, and promised to vote for him and even to do a little 'campaigning', although he wasn't sure what that might entail.

Getting these two groups to trust each other was going to be a work in progress, but it was looking promising. Now he had to test his political skills with Liv. He drove home slowly, trying to think of the best approach. By the time he got home, he still had no good ideas.

She heard his car pull into the garage and came out to meet him. "I'm glad you're home. I owe you an apology - maybe more than one. I am *sooo* sorry!" He put his arms around her, but didn't say a word. He was glad she was apologizing, but he didn't want to jump to any conclusions until he heard what she wanted to apologize *for*, so he let her continue.

"I'm not going to make any excuses, but I would like to explain. I owe you that much! You were right, I did see Sandra as the daughter I never had. I was getting very comfortable with that idea, until she turned on me. I didn't know what to say to her! I was very upset, but I couldn't determine what it was that upset me most. I didn't want to see her in pain, but I also felt a lot of pain myself, and I didn't know what to do about it". She paused, but Mike stayed silent.

"I've been thinking about this a lot, and I see now that she acted in an immature fashion. She's young, so she can be excused for that, but I reacted in much the same way! I should have been the adult in the room, but I wasn't. If I were her mother it would be my responsibility to correct her, but I didn't. I've reached the conclusion that it is probably a good thing I didn't have a child. I do not know how to be a mother." She paused again, and this time Mike decided it was time to ease her pain.

"Liv, don't be that hard on yourself. You have no experience with this sort of thing. You can't be a good parent by reading a book. Oh, yeah, there are plenty of books on the subject of parenting, but this is one of those things that you can only learn by doing, and you've never had the opportunity to try before. It's not like you to give up after only one attempt. If you really care about Sandra, be the adult. Try again."

"But what if she rejects me? I'm not her real mother. I know that, and so does she."

"She connected with you once. You filled a need for her, just as much as she did for you. I think you owe it to both of you to try again, but that's just my opinion. Hey, what do I know? I've never been a mother!"

"No, but you were a father. I've seen the pictures on the staircase wall. You had a family. I haven't asked about those pictures. I figured you'd tell me, if it was something you wanted to talk about."

"It's hard to talk about them – that's my son and my daughter and these are my grandchildren. I...I don't know if their still...alive. You have just recently gained a daughter and now you feel you've lost her. I know how that feels. I would do anything to get my family back, but there's nothing I can do. They are too far away, and I blame myself for letting them leave but I wouldn't be a very good father if I had prevented them from making their own choices. Parenting is hard. All you can do is to keep trying. If there's a chance you can get your daughter back, why wouldn't you try?"

"Mike, I do want her back, but I don't want to lose you, too. I was horrible to you yesterday, and I abandoned you this morning when you needed me. Why are you being so kind to me now?"

"I don't know. It must be because I don't want to lose you, either."

Although he was excited about this morning's success, this was not the time to bore her with the details. He'd tell her all about it tomorrow. Getting their life back together was more important than getting a bunch of feuding town's folk to live in peace.

They prepared a nice dinner together and afterward, spent the evening talking about their lives before the blackout. For a few precious hours, they lived as if the disaster had never happened.

*****

Disaster would be a good word to describe what Joshua had experienced. The humiliation of sitting in the center of that room, forced to listen while Mike spoke – while the Elders agreed with nearly everything he said - had been the worst experience of his life! Even his own father, himself an Elder, had turned against him! The only ally he had was his cousin, Sandra. Not that she understood the concepts that separated Joshua and Mike. She was only loyal to Joshua because he had always been loyal to her.

Today was no different. As soon as he arrived home, Sandra brought him a glass of juice and consoled him in her way. "This should never have happened. You should not be treated this way. I am so angry with that Mike. It's all his fault and I told Liv I never wanted to speak with her again!"

"His fault? No, Sandra, it's mine. I overstepped my authority and I have been chastised for it, as I should be."

"But, you said he went behind your back and spoke to the Elders."

"Oh, yes I did say that. I was wrong. I mean, he did speak to them, but apparently he was unaware of their position in the Church. He thought they were merely farmers, and that I was the leader of the Church. I shouldn't fault him for believing that. I gave him reason to, since I acted as if I were in complete control.

His action was not the deviously clever political move I thought it was. I shouldn't have given him credit for being clever. He is intelligent, but not clever."

"Well, he still caused problems. Doesn't he know you are only doing what must be done for the good of everyone?"

"That's the funny thing about all this…he believes *he* is doing what's best for everyone. We see things differently, but he's not an evil man. Despite his radical ideas, he has also suggested the creation of a volunteer fire department, complete with emergency medical responders, and he recommended you as a member of that team! Our differences are ideological, but they are not personal. I was wrong to think they were. You should not take this personally, either. And you should not take it out on Liv. She probably agrees with him, but that shouldn't prevent the two of you from being friends. I'm sorry if I misled you, Sandra. I know you want to support me, but the last thing I want is for you to be hurt by this! I hope you can restore your friendship with Liv."

Chapter 27 – The calm before the storm

There was never anything to do on Sundays. The Mormons were involved in Church activities, and that meant no one to meet with and no plans could be implemented. Lately, that had bothered Mike, but this morning reminded him of the old days when he would savor the chance to sleep in on Sundays without a care. With Liv by his side again, he intended to do just that. They woke later than usual and got out of bed even later than that.

Liv used the last of the eggs to make omelets for 'brunch'. It was much too late to call it breakfast. The meal left them feeling lazy enough to sit outside and relax. After a few minutes, Liv asked how the meeting had gone. That was Mike's cue to share the news.

"They were pretty hard on Joshua, but that's between them. He knew their rules and he broke them. He still blames me, but remember what you said about Sandra acting immature? Well, maybe it runs in their family! I cannot find any common ground with him, but he's just trying to do what he thinks is right. Too bad he's wrong. He's not happy, but he will probably obey them from now on, and they made it clear that they liked my ideas. They even wanted to make me the Mayor!"

"Oh, that's too bad. If they'd made you King I could be your Queen. I don't think there's a title for the female companion of a Mayor."

"Aah, methinks you jest. Maybe you could be the Court Jester."

"Very funny. I didn't know Mayors did stand-up comedy. So when do you assume your new duties?"

"Never. I explained why I see no reason for a government. We're doing just fine on our own. The water plant will be owned by everyone in the community. We will all be shareholders, and I would appreciate it if you would prepare the legal documents to make that official. We are going to have a shareholder meeting to elect a five-member Board of Directors to oversee the operation. I haven't figured out how we're going to count the votes without appearing illegitimate. I suppose if we count them in front of everyone, that will look fair, but I'm on the ballot so I can't count them."

"That's easy. One person from the Mormon group and one from Jake's crew counting the votes together should satisfy everyone."

"Thank you, you're so smart! Okay, let's see...what else happened...Oh yeah. We're putting together a volunteer fire department and an emergency medical response team. Did you know we have two doctors in town? And Sandra has some training as a nurse, so she can assist."

"She'll be very happy about that!"

"I hope so. Maybe that will also make things easier for you and her to get your relationship back on track. Anyway, the next step is to get phone service working. Having help standing by doesn't do much good if no one can call them. Radar says he can't – or doesn't want to, so the Elders are looking for someone with the technical skills needed. I'm sure everyone in town will know all about these things this afternoon, so maybe we'll hear something tomorrow."

"Good, your plans are coming together. Can you just relax until tomorrow? The best news has been us getting back together, and

I don't want to share you with anyone else today."

"Well...if you insist."

Paul Anthony

Chapter 28 – Storm Clouds

The next four weeks were busy ones. Jake's crew worked long hours to fill the demand for solar installations, first at the water plant, and then the fire station. The cell towers didn't require much power and a man by the name of Lewis set up the phone system, converting everyone's cell phones to work together. As people signed up for phone service, many of them ordered small solar systems in order to recharge their new gadgets, and then expanded their system once they realized what they had been missing.

With summer approaching, and the inevitable high temperatures that always accompanied the season, there was a great demand for evaporative coolers, since solar couldn't be relied upon to generate enough power to run the central AC units everyone was accustomed to using. Fortunately, some of the survivors had mechanical skills, so another new business flourished.

Mary and Tom, a couple the teens encountered when they were shutting off water mains, agreed to re-open their restaurant that they had been living in. Winston's wife didn't see herself as a full-blown entrepreneur, but eventually agreed to supply a few pies per week to the restaurant – for a price, of course.

Mike persuaded someone to set up a 'farmers market', renting stalls to the vendors to make shopping easier. Now, instead of having to drive from farm to farm, buyers could shop in one location. This produced more price comparisons and sometimes heated competition, but people were finally getting the idea that it was okay to 'haggle' over price.

Over time, supply and demand had its effects, too, as would be expected in an unregulated economy. Too many farmers were growing wheat. That meant the supply exceeded the demand, and as haggling increased, the going rate for wheat fell. Some farmers realized the benefit of diversifying their crops, to sell something others weren't offering. They prospered while consumers enjoyed more choice and a diverse diet. Before long, the remaining wheat farmers were able to command higher prices for their wheat because as the supply had been reduced, demand increased.

Teenagers found jobs, not always because they wanted to work, but because there was really nothing else to do these days. Some of them were encouraged to seek employment because their smart parents insisted that they pay for their own phones. There was no such thing as Facebook or Twitter, but texting was as popular as it had always been.

The town had finally come together.

It wasn't perfect. A vendor said some of his merchandise had been stolen. There was some talk of forming a police department – an idea floated by Joshua, of course – but the thief was identified and chastised by... *everyone*. Good old fashioned community peer pressure resolved the problem and it was doubtful the perpetrator would ever steal again.

It was as close to perfect as it would likely ever be.

But clouds were forming on the horizon. Radar had been talking to people outside of town on his CB radio without knowing exactly where those people were. As he reported the news from his part of the world, others were adapting some of those ideas in theirs. But today, the chatter was different.

Someone was talking about the arrival of a train! The people on the train were military types and their leader said they were from the new American government. That was causing mixed emotions in that community, since some of the people were relieved to hear that order was being restored, while others were leery of government intervention. Radar called Mike.

"Mike, I got a report of a group claiming to represent a new government. I don't know where this is happening, but it can't be too far from here. My radio doesn't have much range, so it's probably here in Arizona."

"A government, huh? I don't want to jump to conclusions, but from my experience I suspect the government is going to take more than it gives. I hope I'm wrong. Keep me posted."

The next day, Radar reported the latest news from the other community. The government was promising to bring in all sorts of support, but in the meanwhile the men on the train were asking the town to provide housing and food for them. "They might do some good eventually, but for now it looks like your prediction was spot on, Mike"

It was time to consider a plan to defend the town. Mike asked for a meeting with the Elders. Things had been going so well that when Mike had something to say, the Elders assumed it would prove to be good news. They arrived within the hour, accompanied by Joshua. As Bishop, he was included in their discussions, usually as the sole dissenting vote, but Mike didn't mind. It was always worthwhile to hear an opposing view, if only to reinforce the wisdom of the majority opinion.

"Gentlemen, we may have a problem." He told them what he knew so far and said "If there is a legitimate government, we may benefit from that, but we should consider the possibility that it may represent something that we don't want. What if the government wants to confiscate what we've worked so hard to build, just to redistribute it? I believe we should create a Town Militia to demonstrate our ability to defend ourselves against an armed intrusion. I hope that won't be necessary, but we must appear strong in order to improve our bargaining position."

Silence. The concept was too foreign to register. A few of the Elders whispered to Harold, and eventually he spoke. "We are not inclined to fight. Perhaps you can enlist the aid of Jake and his men. They have military experience. We will pay them to protect us, if that becomes necessary."

Before Mike could respond, Joshua jumped from his chair. "You refused my recommendation for a police force, and now you are going to allow Mike to create his own private army! He is using an imaginary threat to promote fear, and using that fear to grab even more power. This is madness!"

Everyone looked at Mike for a response, and he didn't disappoint them.

"I agree with Joshua, although probably not for the reasons he is imagining. You see, Joshua, I have also studied history and Political Science. I recall something Machiavelli said in one of his less popular works. He advised the Romans against sending their own armies or hired mercenaries into foreign battles. Instead, he spoke of the merits of recruiting local people to fight along with them because the local volunteers would be fighting to protect their homes and their families – not just fighting for a paycheck – and they would fight harder. Many years after Machiavelli wrote that, the wisdom of his words was proven when the American colonists defeated the British army".

Joshua was visibly shaken. He wasn't expecting Mike to agree with him. "Then, what are you proposing?"

"I oppose the idea of a standing army, and especially a mercenary army. We must stand together against any outside threat. I have no doubt Jake and his boys would defend our town if asked, but I'd rather ask them to train the rest of us in the basics. A militia is a citizen army. It functions much the same as a volunteer fire department, coming together only when needed. We have accomplished quite a bit together. Let's do this together, too."

Harold looked sheepish as he replied. "I don't want you to think we are shirking our responsibilities. It is just that we don't think we are qualified to be a part of a militia. I'm not sure any of us could actually shoot another human being. I doubt if I could!"

"I hope it doesn't come to that. The primary purpose of armed strength should be as a deterrent. The enemy should be made to think twice before striking. They may not hesitate if they think there will be no resistance. By demonstrating our ability to resist, we will not be seen as an easy target. That thinking was a major factor in the Cold War, and we won."

Surprisingly, Joshua agreed. "I'm certainly not a hawk, but Mike is right about peace through strength. That strategy has been successful throughout history. I also prefer that we don't put too much power in the hands of a few. If we are all members of the militia we have no reason to fear that power. Most of us own rifles or shotguns and know how to use them. We can *appear* strong together. I only ask for assurances that we will not go on the offensive. I will cooperate if we are only talking about defending our town."

"It's not often Joshua and I agree. I hope the rest of you will, too."

It was agreed, and arrangements were made for some training at Jake's rifle range. At the Elders' urgings, everyone participated in military drills over the next few weeks. Mike promised to keep the Elders informed of any news from the other community.

But there was no more news. Radar was unable to raise the other CB radio. The silence seemed ominous. There was no good reason for a benevolent government to shut down communications!

The farmers had hunting rifles and shotguns but most of the city folk didn't, so Jake and his crew 'borrowed' a few supplies from a National Guard armory in Phoenix. Most of the town's folk would stick with their own weapons, but Jake trained those who were unfamiliar with guns how to use a rifle. He also hand-picked a few young men who were willing, and trained them to handle the more sophisticated weaponry he had procured.

So now the militia had two 'branches' – the 'regulars' and the 'irregulars'. Jake's first line of defense – the 'regulars' – were also split into two, Alpha team and Bravo team. The 'irregulars' were mostly for show, but everyone understood that if anything got past the regulars, the rest of the town had better be ready to fight. Jake's crew saw to it that they were as ready as they could be.

Except for the training exercises, life continued to move closer to 'normal'. With water flowing 24/7 and sewage being treated properly, and all of the food supply free of pesticides and other additives, people could feel assured that they were likely to remain healthy. And in case they weren't, the town's two doctors had teamed up to form a medical practice. Sandra and an older woman were their nurses. The fire station was manned by volunteers, and the two trucks and the ambulance were kept ready for any emergency.

Education had been a delicate topic. Some believed the public schools should be re-opened, while others were in favor of home schooling. A compromise of sorts was reached. Parents would assume responsibility for teaching their own children the basics, but all children would attend a few classes each day at the school, where more specialized subjects were taught by those who were most knowledgeable on each topic.

This curriculum included music, art and sciences and there was talk of forming some sports teams, although that proved problematic. There were barely enough children of the same age to form *one* team. Who would they complete against? The town had started out as a small farming community, but had grown to a town of over twenty-thousand people. There had been several schools and organized sports, and competition not only between schools but also with other towns. Now, it was nearly as small as it had been before the building boom. There were less than two-hundred people left. Life in an isolated community had its drawbacks, but on the plus side, it was peaceful.

The question on Mike's mind was…how long could they remain isolated?

Paul Anthony

Chapter 29 – Invasion

The world had become a noisy place before the blackout. It wasn't obvious until most of the noise had stopped.

With the freeways cluttered with wrecked vehicles, the constant rumble of traffic that had been normal background noise was gone. There were no jets or helicopters buzzing overhead. Most of that noise was really not missed. It had been a part of our lives for as long as most of us could remember, but no one liked any of it - except train whistles. Mike missed train whistles.

He wondered why he was thinking of that now, as he lay in bed. And then he realized that he was hearing a train whistle!

What he felt initially was nostalgia. It's an old-fashioned notion, but the idea of trains chugging across the country side seemed to represent a return of civilization. The pleasant thoughts soon turned to trepidation as he remembered that a train was probably bringing the government Radar had warned them about. Could there really be a government finally responding to the crisis after all this time? Mike was reminded of Ronald Reagan's famous words. "The nine scariest words in the English language are *I'm from the government and I'm here to help*".

They had done just fine without government 'help', and Mike didn't think anything beneficial could come from a visit by government bureaucrats. Or it could it be something more sinister! Maybe there *is* no government. This might just be a rogue group claiming legitimacy, but planning to impose martial law. That seemed more likely.

He rose quickly and called the militia leader.

"Hey, Jake, there's a train coming. What do we know about it?"

"Yeah, we heard it and sent out a scouting party. There's a really old engine with a coal car, a tank car, a flat bed and a box car. There's a tarp over something on the flat bed that could be like an anti-aircraft weapon and there's men in uniform riding in the box car".

"Well, we'd better be prepared for the worst, Jake. You know a lot of people are gonna rush out to greet the train - especially the kids". Mike was thinking about how people used to react when the circus came to town a lot of years ago. "How are we gonna protect those folks if it gets ugly?"

"Bravo team is positioning snipers on the roof tops along the tracks. Alpha team will stay out of sight until the train stops, and then cover the perimeter. I figure we can't do anything until it pulls into town. Do we want to launch an attack, or wait and see?"

"Let's wait. They may be friendly, but it doesn't sound likely. Keep everybody out of sight. I don't want to spook our visitors into doing something rash until I have a chance to assess their intentions. If they uncover what's on that flat bed and it turns out to be a weapon, tell both teams to be ready to eliminate anyone who tries to fire it. But tell them to hold their fire until the other side gives the command to fire. That'll be their cue. That way, you won't have to give the order. Meanwhile, let's get the word out to everyone that'll listen that they should be armed".

"Already on that. Word's spreading".

"Good. You and I need to stay on the phone so you can update me with anything Alpha discovers. I've got this earpiece I hate to use, but I'll use it today. You'll do the talking, while I just listen. We don't need to let our visitors know we have the ability to communicate. I'd better get down there to meet the train. I don't want the Bishop to be our spokesman!"

"We'll be ready".

And Mike knew Jake meant it. He and his boys had been training together for over a month, just waiting for a chance to see some action. *"I just hope they're not too trigger-happy"*, Mike muttered to himself as he got dressed for the meeting he'd hoped would never be necessary.

"Who would have thought I'd be driving into town to meet a train! Life sure throws some interesting curve balls" Mike said to Plato, who looked up with his usual calm, all-knowing expression. Nothing fazed Plato. Sometimes Mike wished he could feel as confident as his dog looked.

Liv was getting dressed. "I'll be ready in no time, I promise", she said as she slipped into a pair of jeans.

"No you won't. This could get ugly. I want you to stay here. Plato will keep you company."

She stopped and glared at him. "I'm a part of the militia, too, remember? And I thought we had already settled this thing about you telling me what to do."

"Yeah, you are part of the militia, and I out-rank you so I DO get to tell you what to do. Stay here. That's an order Private." In a softer tone he added "I mean it, Liv. Stay here... please." She sat on the bed, a pout starting to form around the corners of her mouth. She was angry, but she let him kiss her. This was an argument she knew she couldn't win so she hugged him and said "You'd better come back alive, or so help me, I'll kill you!" And she let him go.

He arrived before the train. Good. People were milling around, trying to get a first look as its whistle grew louder. The Bishop was among them, of course, looking like a politician waiting to cut a ceremonial ribbon. What were these people thinking? Why were they so sure this was cause for celebration? Damn optimists. They might get themselves killed, but they'd probably die with smiles on their faces.

Well, he needed to ensure that no one died today.

A careful look around was less than reassuring. He had told Jake to keep his people out of sight, and now he wished they hadn't done such a good job of it. Well, he'd just have to trust that they were ready. Just then, Jake's voice came over the phone. *"Four men got off the train before it reached town. They've been, uh, neutralized"*. Well, that was a good piece of information to have.

The train stopped right in front of the crowd. It was show time.

Three men stepped off the train, looking very military in their camo-style fatigues, but they weren't wearing any patches Mike could recognize. The clothes looked authentic, but they could have come from an Army surplus store. Two of the men had automatic weapons that didn't look Army-issue. The third man had a standard-issue side arm in his holster and a... *sword!?!* These were definitely not regular Army.

Mike stepped forward a few paces before the Bishop could, and greeted the three. "Hello. Welcome to our town. What can we do for you?"

Smiling broadly, the man with the sword said "I'm Colonel Hall with the new American government. By order of the President, we have come to protect your town from the rebels. You'll be safe as long as we're here. You will provide us with food, water, housing and a building we can use as my headquarters. In return, we will guard your town".

"We'll be happy to share food and water, but first, tell us about this new government. Where is it headquartered? And who is it you're protecting us from? We haven't seen any 'rebels'. What makes you think there's any danger here?"

"What's your name, mister?" The Colonel was no longer smiling.

"Sorry, that was rude of me. My name is Mike. Now how about answering my questions?" Mike said with a smile as phony as the Colonel's had been.

"I'll fill you in on all the details you need to know in due time, but first you'll have to show me some good faith by complying with my orders. Otherwise, I might be inclined to think you are one of the rebels". The Colonel was trying very hard to put a smile back on his face, but not quite succeeding.

"Well Colonel, I've never heard of your new American government, and I'm pretty sure none of us voted for your President, so I don't see any reason why we would want to take orders from you". Mike had given up any pretense of smiling. "So here's what we'll do. We'll give you fresh water and ask that you get back on your train and move on".

As Mike finished that sentence, Jake's voice cut in. *"Careful, Mike. Alpha has been taking a closer look at the train from the*

other side while everybody's looking in your direction, and that
coal car is almost empty. I'd say this guy is highly motivated to
make a stand right here and now. Also, there are about a dozen
soldiers in the box car and they're heavily armed".

Shit! By offering the guy an option, I just reminded him that he
doesn't have any! This isn't going well. No more Mr. Nice guy – it's
time to talk tough. "Look Colonel, no one needs to get hurt today.
But if you push us, keep in mind you're outnumbered and
outgunned. If it comes to a fight, you will lose".

"Hah! You don't think I would come here with just the three of
us, do you?" Then he barked an order and his men jumped out of
the box car, weapons ready. "All of my men are trained soldiers
and I have a battalion surrounding this town of yours. You and
your farmer friends with your little rifles are no match for us.
Besides, I doubt if your town folks have the guts to shoot anything
bigger than a squirrel.

Mike's mind was racing. If he is looking at "farmers with rifles"
that means the town folk behind him were standing their ground.
That's good. Hopefully, they also had the good sense to get the
women and children off the street. Mike wanted to be sure, but
he didn't dare turn around. He had to face the Colonel and look
confident, even if he didn't feel confident.

Mike let out a hearty laugh. "A battalion? You mean the four
men that jumped off the train at the last bend before you got
here? They've been, *uh*, detained. Like I said, you are
outnumbered and outgunned".

The Colonel seemed a little rattled by that news, but he kept up
his bravado and gave the order to man the 'big guns'. Two
soldiers climbed on the flat bed and removed the tarps that had

covered two machine guns. Jake's voice was in Mike's ear again. *"We just got a peek in the boxcar. They have prisoners in chains."* Well, that settled it. There would be no negotiating.

Mike said "Are you declaring war, Colonel?"

"You give me no choice. What's about to happen is your fault. *Men! Fire when ready!*"

The air exploded with the sound of gun fire. Mike and the Colonel continued to stare at each other, neither of them flinching, neither willing to show weakness.

And then, the shooting stopped. The Colonel looked....*confused*. None of the town folks had fallen! How could his men have missed ...*everyone?* And why weren't his men still firing? As the answers slowly dawned on him, he reluctantly broke off his staring contest and turned to survey the carnage behind him.

As the Colonel turned, Mike pulled his Glock from its holster while explaining "Everyone here is part of the Town militia. Some of them are farmers, but some of them are ex-special forces. We positioned snipers on the rooftops before you arrived. They've had your men in their sights since you got here, waiting patiently as only well-trained soldiers can. We also had another team follow you in. They were the ones that intercepted your 'battalion'. That team had you surrounded, and they also waited for orders". Mike allowed a minute for all that to sink in, and then he continued. "Now here's the best part. *You* gave the order to fire! They responded to *your* command! All of this blood is on *your* hands".

When the Colonel turned to face Mike again, he also had his service revolver drawn, but the barrel was pressed against his own chin. "War is hell, especially when you lose". Those were his last words before his head exploded.

It was over and Mike was tired. He felt like he had been standing there for hours, although it couldn't have been more than fifteen minutes. People were crowding around him, patting him on the back and trying to shake his hand. Someone called him a hero. *A hero?* He didn't feel heroic. He just felt tired.

That's how it usually happens. Heroes aren't people who set out to do heroic deeds. They are people who do what has to be done, reacting without a plan, acting out of necessity. It only looks heroic to all the people who *didn't* act.

People need heroes, but they also need to feel they could be one, too. That's why fans cheer for their favorite football team, so they can feel like they are part of that team even though they're probably not in any shape to play. These people wanted to feel like they deserved to share in today's victory. Mike knew he had to give them that assurance. And, why shouldn't he? After all, they hadn't run away. They deserved to be told how heroic they had been.

But there were other matters that had to take precedence. Alpha team was picking up weapons and making sure there were no live bodies attached to any of them. Mike thanked Jake and promised to call him back. The prisoners in the boxcar needed help, and Mike had to hang up on Jake to call for medical assistance. The next call he placed was to Liv. Then, he climbed up on the flat bed and made an impromptu speech to thank all the 'heroes' that had gathered around. "Together, we saved our town. Our medical team is treating the Colonel's prisoners – all women. I don't have to tell you why he had them in chains. If we had failed here, most likely our men would be dead and our women would be taking their place in that boxcar. You have all acted bravely by standing your ground and I am proud of all of you!"

Spirits were high and a celebratory party was brewing, but Mike slipped away. He just wanted to go home to Liv.

*****

Liv had heard the shots, and it seemed she would never be able to catch her breath! The shooting stopped, and she exhaled. What now? She tried to call Mike, but it went straight to voice mail. He could be on the phone or...

She was on her way out to her car when her phone rang. It was Mike, and her world was no longer falling apart. She said she would be there right away, but Mike said he was coming home. She waited like a dutiful wife - or as a dutiful Private.

When Mike got home, he described the events of the day in the fewest possible words. He told her there were prisoners on the train, but didn't mention they were all female, no doubt sex slaves. Likewise, he assured her that the enemy had been stopped without mentioning that they had been slaughtered. The details were too gory. All that mattered was that they were safe. She'd probably hear more from others in the coming days, but he didn't want to trouble her today - or relive it himself. He just wanted to enjoy some peace and quiet with the woman he loved. He felt certain that he had earned that.

Apparently, that opinion wasn't shared by everyone. Harold called. The Elders wanted to meet to discuss Mike's handling of the situation. Mike assured Harold he would be happy to discuss it

– *tomorrow!* He was taking the rest of the day off.

Chapter 30 – The day after

The next morning, Mike prepared to face the firing squad. Well, not literally, of course, but he was certain some sparks were going to fly. It would be like the typical couch-potatoes quarterbacking after the game was over. They'd all have their own opinions of what he should have done, in spite of the fact that none of them had a clue or the guts to do anything themselves when something *needed* to be done.

He had already replayed the scene in his head. He'd made the right call whether they agreed or not, but he would explain his thought processes to them anyway. He had considered trying to capture the enemy alive, but that would have meant giving them a chance to shoot back, and he didn't want any of the town's people getting shot. Besides, if they took prisoners, what would they do with them? Who would guard them? Who would feed them? No, the only options were convincing them to leave or eliminating them. He had offered the Colonel the chance to leave. If Mike hadn't taken the actions he had, the town's men would be dead and its women would wish they were.

Let them complain. It wasn't like they could change the outcome. They would have to accept it as it was. The fact that they were still alive to argue about it should be evidence that he had been right. How could anyone argue in favor of a different outcome?

He would be facing this alone. He didn't want Liv to be there, in case it proved to be humiliating, so he was grateful when she said she was going to Sandra's.

As he approached the church, he thought back to the first time he had been summoned to a meeting of the Elders. Would they expect him to sit in the lone seat in the middle of the floor as Joshua had been forced to do?

He opened the front door to the church and entered cautiously. The Elders rose from their seats and ...*applauded!*

Caught completely by surprise, Mike stood in the doorway, not sure what his next move should be. He did manage to glance around enough to notice there was no solitary chair waiting for him. He had been wrong about them, and was not the least bit upset with being wrong this time. So, if this wasn't going to be an inquisition, why was he here?

They escorted him to a seat next to the podium. That's when he realized that Liv was sitting in the next seat. She was in on this, whatever it was! Harold approached the podium to make what must have been a prepared speech since he was fumbling with a stack of index cards. The speech, like most of those types of speeches, droned on for what seemed like an eternity. Mike was half-listening. Apparently, it had been decided that the train should be left where it was and a plaque be created to commemorate the battle. It would stand as a reminder of...Mike's attention was waning.

Finally reaching the end of his speech and *finally* getting to the point of it all, Harold declared that, although the town had no formal government, Mike was to be the town's 'Honorary Mayor'.

And that was how an anarcho-Libertarian became a pseudo-bureaucrat.

Well, they could call him whatever they wanted to call him. He was still a businessman. Every monetary exchange that occurred in this town whether it was buying and selling or paying employees, had to pass through Mike's 'virtual bank'. He was too busy to pretend to be a politician.

But, just for today, he'd be the person they wanted him to be. Tomorrow, life would go back to 'normal' – or what had become normal lately.

Chapter 31 – ...And all the days to come

Mike's business took up a lot of his time. Liv's concerns that he would be moody with nothing to do were unfounded. He had too much to do! The paperwork (actually, data entries in computer spreadsheets) was becoming too much for one person to do, so Mike interviewed some applicants and hired two for clerical positions. Unlike the fiasco that occurred at the water treatment plant, Mike hired 'apprentices' that had some appropriate skills and something resembling a work ethic!

The 4% transaction fees were amounting to a sizeable sum, and Mike – not being a member of the Church – wasn't expected to tithe. He believed everyone should be charitable, so he let it be known that he would provide for the financial needs of the Fire Department. Whenever they were called upon to fight a fire or respond to a medical emergency, Mike would pay the responders. After all, serving the community meant the volunteers would be taking time out from whatever they usually did to support their families. Someone should compensate them for that, and since there was no government and no taxation to support one, Mike took it upon himself to fill the gap. He also re-opened the public library and paid a librarian. So instead of the 'Mayor' *collecting* a paycheck, he would pay for municipal services. Finally, a public servant that served the public! That was the sort of government Mike could support!

Joshua was pleasantly surprised to hear Mike's plan. They would never agree entirely, but there was less friction between them than there had been, and that cease-fire was helping Liv and Sandra renew their friendship.

Sandra enjoyed her new responsibilities as a nurse and Liv was busy providing legal services. Most of the town's adult population had found gainful employment, either as merchants or as employees. The former seemed very happy with their new lives, but some of the latter had already begun to complain about working conditions and/or insufficient compensation. There was some talk about forming a union.

Mike thought it was ironic. When some of these people were completely dependent upon the good graces of others for everything, they didn't dare complain. Now that they were given the opportunity to improve their lot – and they were definitely better off than they had been – they complained. Some people preferred being taken care of, even if it meant barely getting by, over being responsible for their own well-being.

Mike struggled with this thought. He couldn't decide if his instincts were morally correct, but he wondered...If Joshua hadn't fed these people, they would have probably perished as so many others did. The only survivors would be those who were self-reliant. Would the world be a better place if 'survival of the fittest' had been left unchecked? In this case, 'fittest' didn't mean those who were physically strongest, but those who were better prepared, smarter in some ways and...well, *responsible*.

This was not a subject he'd be willing to discuss with just anyone, but he thought he might talk with Liv about it.

Life was pretty good, all things considered. The basic necessities like food, water and heating and cooling were adequate, even if the dietary choices weren't as varied as they used to be and they needed to use evaporative coolers, since it wasn't possible to generate enough electricity for central air conditioning.

Entertainment choices were limited. The movie theater was re-opened, but no one was making new blockbuster movies. There was no television, but there was a local radio station that broadcast a mix of different music styles and what little local news there was.

Mike had two competent employees, which allowed him to spend less time working and more time with Liv, who had less work herself, now that most of the contracts needed had already been written.

It was another Sunday. While most of the town's populace attended Church, Mike and Liv enjoyed their time together, talking and relaxing from their work week. This Sunday, Liv started their chat with a question.

"What do you think life will be like twenty years from now?"

With a grin, Mike said "You mean aside from the fact that we'll be twenty years older? Let's see...I haven't done the math, but I'd estimate only about 25% of our current population is 18 or over. In ten years, more than half of them will be in their child bearing years so, twenty years from now the population will likely be three to four times what it is now. That could cause some growing pains, with a lot more mouths to feed but not that many more people old enough to raise food."

"I don't know, Mike, are you sure that will be a problem? For years, we heard about population growth increasing at a rate that would overpower our ability to produce food, but we found more efficient ways of growing crops. Don't you think our farmers will find ways to increase their yield?"

"You're probably right, Liv. And we're both assuming all the population increase will come from within. Historically, people have migrated from Mexico looking for a better life. That has been going on since before Arizona was a state and it may happen again, although they may not get any further north than the Tucson area — assuming there are surviving communities around Tucson."

"Oh, yeah. What about people coming here from other parts of Arizona, or from other states?"

"I think that's less likely. Most of the population of the state was in the greater Phoenix area, and most of them are gone. If there are other communities like ours, those people will probably stay where they are or attempt to move north. Some of our own people may, too, because it's been a long time since we've had fresh meat. I don't miss it, but some people do. They may want to go north to hunt."

"I wouldn't want to make the trip, but if anyone else did, they could make a killing — pardon the pun — if they could bring the meat back and sell it here!"

"But going north could be risky. The population of the towns up north were always small, but I'd bet a larger percentage of those folks survived. There may be more people there now than there are here, and they might not take too kindly to intruders. And I doubt any of them would want to come here. Wait, some of my neighbors were going north right after the blackout. I don't know if they ever got there, but if they did, they may try to come back. Still, there is the possibility that some trade routes could be established."

Liv jumped up. "Oh, no! I can hear the wheels turning in that busy little brain of yours, Mike. Please tell me you are not thinking of travelling north to set up more businesses."

"No, I am quite content to stay right here with you. Besides, trade with any other group of people will be difficult. Remember, we don't have a currency. Our 'money' is only good here. I don't foresee a global economy developing anytime soon – or ever, actually. There may never be another United States, either, and maybe that's a good thing. The larger the geopolitical entity, the more likely it is for someone to create some sort of central planning. I hope we don't make that mistake again."

Liv's smile demonstrated her sarcasm when she said "So we're pioneers charting a new path for humanity."

"Well... I guess you could call us pioneers with benefits. There's no question we are taking advantage of a lot of infrastructure that was built before we became 'pioneers'. But we were taxpayers, so we paid for most of that infrastructure, and it will last longer with fewer people using it. For instances, our roads may need some repair in time, but there are a lot fewer cars and no large delivery trucks to wear them out and, although I see our population expanding exponentially, it will be a long time before we'll need to build more houses."

"Mike, it sounds like you want everything to stay simple. It has been my experience that things always get more complicated than we want them to be."

"Yes. I was thinking a while ago that Joshua, with the best of intentions, helped some people to survive that wouldn't have on their own. Those are the same people who are grumbling about having to work. They want others to take care of them. They're trying to unionize, so that someone will. When I thought of that, I was angry, but now I realize that if it didn't happen now it would probably happen with the next generation or the one after that. There will always be people who can't stand on their own. So, yes, I would like everything to stay the way it is but I know it won't. I will, however, do everything I can to keep things this way for the remaining years I have left."

"I'm seeing a different side of you, Mike. I thought you were an optimist, but your predictions seem pretty pessimistic."

"An optimist is often disappointed. A pessimist is never disappointed, but never experiences any joy. I prefer to think of myself as a realist. By being realists, we've managed to create a pretty good life without the disappointments unrealistic expectations bring. It will be up to future generations to keep this 'good life' for themselves – or change it in ways that suit them. I'm sure things will change, but time will tell if those changes make life better or worse. We don't have a lot of things we used to have, but how many of those things would we want back?"

"I don't know…more entertainment options might be nice."

"Is that all you miss? I would think there are some technological advances that will have to be re-discovered. We're using the fuel that is available. Someday, someone will have to remember how to refine oil – or find a new method of transportation! But I don't miss the crowds or taxes or junk mail or telemarketing calls or political campaigns or…"

"Okay, I get it! There were a lot of things that were more annoying than pleasant. Things will change, and some of those things may crop up again. We can't stop innovation."

"I wouldn't want to. I just hope people will refrain from thinking they know best and insisting that everyone else conform to their way of thinking. I suppose Joshua would say I've been guilty of that. I am responsible for the type of economy we have, but I tried to persuade people to join in. I didn't force anyone to participate, and that's the difference. At least, I hope that counts for something. Everyone is free to live their life as they choose, as long as exercising their freedom doesn't prevent others from exercising their own."

"If we can teach *that* to the next generation, life will probably be good for many years to come!"

www.ingramcontent.com/pod-product-compliance
Lightning Source LLC
Chambersburg PA
CBHW061140170626
46809CB00003B/935